LUNA STATION
QUARTERLY

Issue 037 | March 2019

Editor-in-Chief

Jennifer Lyn Parsons

Editors

Linda Codega • Caroljean Gavin
Shel Graves • Cathrin Hagey • Dana Mele
Kimberly Osgood • Gô Shoemake

LUNA STATION PRESS
NEW JERSEY

First Paperback Edition March 2019
ISBN: 978-1-949077-06-3

Luna Station Quarterly publishes short fiction on March 1st, June 1st,
September 1st, and December 1st. For more information and submission
guidelines, please visit our website at lunastationquarterly.com

LUNA STATION PRESS

For Luna Station Press

Creative Director - Tara Quinn Lindsey
Editor-in-Chief & Founder - Jennifer Lyn Parsons

www.lunastationpress.com

CONTENTS

Editorial

Jennifer Lyn Parsons

Jennifer Lyn Parsons is a writer, programmer, and maker. With influences ranging from Laura Ingalls Wilder to Jim Jarmusch, her tales feature a rare physicality with details that feel hand-carved. When not writing code or prose, she is also the editor-in-chief of the venerable Luna Station Quarterly. She finds joy in video games, comics books, discovering music new and old, and making things out of wool, paper, and wood.

I can think of few better examples of how elastic the concept of time can be than when I look back on the last nine years. It is not an inevitability for any publication to last this long. That timeframe becomes more fragile if they publish short fiction, and doubly so if they have the audacity to focus on a particular niche.

Of course even as I wrote that I bristled at the thought of women-identified writers being a "niche". More than half the population of the world is hardly what I would call a minority. Perhaps one day that won't feel so untrue.

But back to those nine years we've got tucked under our belts. They feel long, especially the last couple and yet, at the same time, they flew. One of the authors who's story you will be reading shortly was too young to read the first issue when it came out and now she's old enough to be sharing her own writing with you all. The early issues were wobbly things that required a fair bit of duct tape and peanut butter to hold them together and now they're these flourishing creatures who stand strong on their own. Somewhere in there I got older and grayer, though I don't feel much of it other than in the hard-won wisdom I carry with me. I replaced a lot of the fucks I used to give with wisdom. You can only carry so much and something had to go, ya know?

I started LSQ with a goal of supporting women-identified writers who were not getting a chance elsewhere. When I look at what we've done to support , that bears out. Over the years I've had the pleasure of giving a number of folks their first publishing credits. Many of them have gone on to publish more stories and novels and are now making their living writing. A few have even joined the staff of this very magazine.

Along with looking back, we're also looking forward, like any self-respecting speculative fiction magazine should. What are the possibilities yet before us? The next year will be exciting and interesting, a landmark year for us here at LSQ. Along with the wisdom we've gathered, there is confidence gained in reaching year ten. It's not about getting comfortable though, in fact it's the opposite. It's about knowing where the edges of things are now, including some boundaries that are starting to feel a little snug. We're old hands at this now, but that doesn't mean our tasks are taken for granted.

Our first nine years have been about learning who we are, how we do the things we do, laying foundation that's built to last. Year ten will be about reflecting a bit on all that has come before and then priming the rockets for the next leap. We'll look back to see all the things that have worked and celebrate, and the things that didn't and recalibrate.

I look forward to sharing this very special year with you all. I hope you join me as we give thanks for all that has happened to get us here. More importantly, I hope you stay and even pull your chair a little closer to the fire. We're a thousand bright stars in a shared galaxy right now, I'd love to bring you all into our orbit so we can shine all the brighter.

"Spark joy" is a phrase that is on many people's minds lately. The heart of that phrase is a guide for finding the things in your life that have meaning, and bring true value to your life and then being grateful for those things in an open, honest and authentic way.

I hope the stories we have been telling all these years spark joy for you. More than that, may the stories we have yet to share continue to delight, encourage, uplift, and make you feel things in deep, meaningful ways that enrich your life.

Thank you for the last nine years. I look forward to thanking you again a decade from now and can't wait to see what the seeds we're planting will yield. Together lets sow for prosperity, generosity, community, and wonderful stories.

Alright, year ten starts now!

L S Q | 037

Two Monsters Down in the Dark

E. H. Mann

E. H. Mann lives and writes in Melbourne, Australia. Some of their other stories have appeared in Mother of Invention (Twelfth Planet Press, 2018) and Fabled Journey (Remastered Words, 2018). By day she works in customer service, volunteers as an asexuality advocate, and wrestles with brain weasels and concepts of gender. They want to be a writer when they grow up, but may not be willing to wait that long.

I'm shoveling gold into my bag by the fistful when Benji says, "I don't like it."

The cave is so cold my fingers are going numb even inside their cloth wraps. I sniff, but my nose keeps trying to drip anyway, just like the water goes on dripping from the pointy rocks on the ceiling.

Benji's rucksack is still empty. He keeps on: "Something's not right. This is supposed to be a dragon's lair."

"You said we wouldn't see the dragon," I point out.

"Trust me, we won't see the dragon—that monster's well dead. But if this is a dragon's lair, where's the rest of it?" He raises his lantern and waves it around the cave. It's about as big as our place, but that's not very big.

"The beast's supposed to have laired here a century at least," says Benji. "Don't tell me it spent a hundred years in this stinking hole."

I like the smell here—faintly mineral behind the tang of the oil in our lamps—but I don't say that out loud. Benji doesn't expect an answer.

"And another thing: it's supposed to have cracked open two temples and a bank back in its raiding days—liberated gold sovereigns by the thousands. This is a tiny fraction of that. So what happened to the rest? What do you think—does a dragon go shopping?"

He grins at me, but I don't feel like laughing.

Benji goes pacing the walls of the cave, ignoring the money, ignoring the big hole we came in through, looking at everything else close up. Where his light moves on, it leaves darkness behind.

There were glow-bugs on the walls when we got here, tiny points of green I could only see when I looked at them sideways, but we've shone too much light around now and they've quit their glowing. The darkness of the cave isn't like the darkness of the city at night. It's true black, all-devouring.

We shouldn't be here.

"This is plenty of money," I say as Benji prowls. "It'll keep us for years, if we're careful."

"Careful?" he scoffs. "If we live like paupers, you mean. Don't you want your dresses, Squirt? Don't you want me to have my trinkets?"

Benji loves showing off when we've got money—gold on his fingers and in his ears. The rings only last as long as the money does, and then he has to trade them.

I scowl down at my work. Benji knows I want those dresses. Proper dresses, made by a real tailor, that I can wear to market so maybe people won't whisper and stare so much. I've been making my own dresses since I was old enough to hold a needle, but even if I get lucky sometimes and can buy decent fabric, they still look like something a child would sew. Benji says my hands are too big for delicate work.

I want those dresses. But not as much as I want us to get out of here.

"We don't know the dragon's dead," I try.

"Don't *worry* so, Ellie," says Benji with a laugh. "That monster's been going in and out of this hole for decades. Now no one's seen scale nor tooth of it in a month. Whaddya think it's doing, sleeping out the winter like a bear? Hey, give me a hand here."

He's peering up into the dark, lifting his lantern towards something too high for him to see. My brother is a short man, stunted by a childhood of never enough to eat and a broken leg we couldn't afford to have set right.

I put down my bag and go pick Benji up, lifting him onto my shoulders as easy as a father lifting a child.

"Hah!" he crows. "There *is* a hole there! How'd you miss that, Squirt? I thought trolls were supposed to have good night-sight!"

He's teasing me. Trollbloods don't have any real troll blood—it's just what normal folks call people like me because we're big and strong and slow of thought and speech. Brawn before brains, Benji says. He takes after our mother.

Benji scrambles off my shoulders, up to a rocky ledge.

"This is it! Big enough for a dragon to fit through, and it's worn—you can see where the beast's been back and forth. It must have left a little of its hoard here as a decoy—a clever monster, then. But not clever enough for us! Come on!"

He disappears from view, trusting me to follow. I hear his boots scrabbling over rock, getting quieter and further away.

I stand still.

I know I shouldn't. I always do what Benji tells me. I stand still anyway, even though it makes my guts twist.

More scrabbling. Benji's head reappears. "Ellie? What're you doing down there? Let's go!"

I take a deep breath, feeling the heat rise in my cheeks. "No."

He holds out his lantern to stare down at me.

"Whaddya mean, no?" he says, and now the hard edges are creeping into his voice.

I stare at a spine of rock sticking out of the ground, slick and slimy with water. If I look at his face I'll lose my nerve. "We got enough here, Benji. We should just take it and go." Even to me it sounds like a child's whine.

"Oh ho! You want to tell me what to do now, is that it? Well isn't that great!" I hate it when his voice gets like this, loud and hard and a little bit sing-song. "Can't get a word out of you when I'm planning this job, but now we're here, ohhhh, Ellie's taking charge!"

Even without looking, I can see his face, thin and sharp and angry.

"Useless muscle, you are. Won't break down a door, won't rough up a guy, won't even join the fighting rings—"

"Don't like fighting," I mutter, hating how sulky it sounds.

"You like killing pigs well enough!"

I hate killing pigs. They struggle, and they scream like banshees. I hate the fear in their eyes when they look at me, before my knife does its work.

I don't want to hurt them, but there aren't many places will give work to a trollblood. The butchers down The Shambles like that I can pin a hog all by myself, and they like that I don't mind when their boys play jokes on me, so they give me plenty of work. The money's OK—not like what Benji brings in, but enough to keep him from fussing when I won't help out with his jobs.

"Give me the bag," says Benji.

Startled, I look up. The lantern-light shadows make his face hard to read.

"Don't just stare at me, troll-skull! Give me your bag." He sticks out a hand.

I can't figure out what he's planning, and my guts are twisting right up, but I pass the half-full sack of gold up to him. I always do what Benji tells me.

"OK," he says. "Now fuck off."

My stomach drops. "What?"

"You heard me. You're so smart, you clearly don't need my help. So fuck off."

"You mean go home?" It sounds stupid even as I say it.

"Hah! No. You're so keen to make the decisions around here, I reckon you can look after yourself now. Hey, I know! You could go be a monster-hunter!"

"That's not funny," I tell him, feeling my throat tighten.

Our dad was a monster-hunter. It's one line of work where a troll-blood can get rich, and people like having you around even.

I don't remember our dad.

I was only little when we came to Abercoombe to slay their dragon. It had lived under these hills since there was only a little town down in the valley, and it left people alone even when the town became a city and spread decade by decade all the way up into the hills. Then all of a sudden it started raiding temples for gold.

No one knew why it started. No one knew why it stopped again just a few months later. But in between, our dad went down this hole to fix it for good, and he never came back out.

When his money ran out, our mum did what she could to look after us, but she'd never learned to be anything but a monster-hunter's wife. A year later she was gone too. We told people she'd died of a broken heart. As Benji liked to say, no one wants to give money to orphans whose mum died of the purse-rot.

I don't remember much of her either. I was only little.

Benji remembers.

"Twelve years I've looked out for you," he says. His voice is quiet now, but no less hard. "Twelve years I've kept us both alive in a world that couldn't care two bits if we wound up dead in a ditch. Twelve years scraping and scrounging and working my fingers to the bone to keep a roof over your head. Well, no more. You think you're so smart, you can take care of yourself."

He turns his back and disappears again, dragging my bag behind him. It goes clinking and rattling over the rocks, getting quieter and quieter, and then I can't hear it at all.

My shoulders are tight, my hands clenched up in fists.

I could do it. I could take care of myself. The butchering money is enough to keep me, if I'm careful with it. Or I could find a better job, so I don't have to kill pigs anymore. Benji thinks all I'm good for is my strength, but Benji doesn't know the whole of me.

The only light now is the circle around my lantern. The glowbugs haven't come back, and I miss the comfort of their soft constellations. My fingernails are digging sharp into my palms.

But finding a new place to live or a better job, that means talking to people. Abercoombe is full of them—quick people, sharp people, who look at me with impatience or with fear and won't wait around while I try to find my words. People who call me worse things than troll-skull when I mess up, and sometimes even when I don't. How will I get anyone to listen to me without Benji to do the talking?

The only sounds left are my sniffing, over and over, and the quiet drip, drip of water. A freezing drop hits the back of my neck, making me shiver and hunch.

And Benji is walking away from me, off into the dark. Walking towards the dragon.

I pull myself up into the hole, scramble through a tight tunnel, until the space opens up and I start running.

I've only gone a little way through the next cavern when I see light ahead. I stumble around some rocks, and there's Benji, leaning against the wall.

He smirks. "Glad you decided to join me."

I say nothing.

"And another thing," says Benji, "Konrad was offering good money for you to work at the gaming house! You wouldn'ta had to fight or anything, just stand around looking menacing when people don't wanna hand over their money, and keep your trap shut if the watchmen come 'round. What was wrong with that, huh?"

We're still walking through the caves. I'm following Benji, and Benji is following the path worn smooth through each cavern by the dragon's belly. This far in there aren't glow-bugs, just darkness and cold and dripping damp, and the sack of gold bouncing against my shoulder, and a nasty feeling burning in my throat where all the things I want to say to Benji are stuck like hot peppers. It's an old, familiar feeling, and I hate it.

Benji won't shut up.

"That other trollblood they got, he makes ten shillings a week. A week, Ellie! You take that kind of work, you'd be bringing in more than me half the time! But noooo, you didn't like that either."

I know why he does this. He's had to look out for us ever since we were small. When we were starving brats without family or home, and I was too little to be much good for anything, he used his clever brain and his clever words to bring in money any way he could think of. That was his whole life, thinking up ways to keep us. Small wonder money's so important to him still, even now we mostly have enough.

This is how it's always been. Even after I outgrew him and kept on growing. Benji's the smart one, the normal one, the one people will talk to. He's only looking out for his poor, slow, trollblood sister.

Some of the pointy rocks have fallen down off the ceiling here and busted up the rocks that used to stick up from the ground. The floor is a mess of rubble. My shoulders are bunched up tight.

"I swear, I don't know what goes through your skull—" says Benji, and then he disappears.

I throw myself forward, reaching for my brother as the floor swallows him up, but there's a broken rock sticking up and I smash my head on it hard. Lights flash behind my eyes and the ground knocks the wind out of me, and for a second I don't know who I am or where I am or what's going on.

When the lights in my head fade, it's so dark I can't tell if my eyes are open or closed. The blackness feels like drowning in ink. I'm lying on the cave floor with my left arm braced against rock and nothing at all under my chest, and my right arm is stretched way down into the nothing, and my hand is closed tight around coarse fabric.

I can hear muffled swearing below me, and somewhere, way, way below that, the quiet sound of water running.

"Benji?"

"OK," he says in a tight voice. "OK. Don't move, Ellie."

"I won't."

He starts to wriggle around in my grip. He's not heavy, but I can't help imagining him slipping by accident right out of his coat. Then I feel hands on my wrist, clinging hard, and he tells me to get up.

I lift Benji out of the hole, and he fumbles around on the ground and finds my lantern to relight. It takes him longer than usual to strike a spark, the flint rattling hard against the firesteel. His own lantern is long gone, down to the river, somewhere far below us in the dark. In the lamplight, his eyes are very big.

He looks at me, and his eyes get bigger. The light glistens on red splashes on the rocks.

"Shit," says Benji. "You OK?"

My face is wet. I put my hand to my head, and it comes away covered in blood. Lots of blood, like I've just cut a pig's throat.

In an instant, I'm a child again. My voice comes out high: "Benji?"

My brother darts over with the lantern, and looks close at my head. He touches my forehead here and there, stares at my eyes real close, makes me tell him how many fingers he's holding up, and then he grabs my hand and presses it hard over a spot that throbs.

"It's OK, Squirt, it's just a cut. You'll be OK. Head wounds bleed like a devil, is all. You keep that pressure on there." He's tearing big strips off his shirt hem. He folds one up over the cut, then wraps the other around and around my head.

His hands are gentle. I mop at the blood on my face with my coat sleeve, and don't look at him.

Benji finishes bandaging me, wipes his hands on his trousers, and smoothes back my hair. "Hey," he says, trying to meet my eyes. "You know I wasn't actually gonna leave you back there, right? I knew you'd come after me. I waited for you."

Hot peppers in my throat. I stare down at my coat sleeve, red and sticky. If I don't clean that up soon, it will stain.

"Hey, c'mon, don't be like that. I talk a lot of horse-shit—you know that, right?" He squeezes my shoulder. "You pissed me off and I acted out, but you know I don't mean anything by it. I always look out for you, right, Squirt? Don't I always look out for you?"

He sounds so hurt that I have to look at him. I meet his eyes, and they're still the eyes of the boy that used to pluck feathers from my ear to make me laugh, when I was little and my belly hurt from hunger.

"I know," I tell him. It's true. I wouldn't be alive if not for him.

He flashes me a big smile, and then he's up and walking around, quick and jerky, like he's got fire in his veins. "Whoof—that got my heart racing!" he laughs, too loud. He's not looking at me anymore.

There are words building up behind my teeth, pushing to be let out, but I'm still trying to find the right order for them when suddenly Benji crouches and mutters, "What's this, now?"

He holds up the edge of a big piece of sack-cloth, stained dark with soot.

"This is why I didn't see that hole! It was over the top!"

He gets up and starts looking all around. "And these rocks here, they didn't fall on their own. Someone knocked them down so we'd have to walk around them, over where the hole is. Not a complicated trap, but clever enough if you're not looking for it..."

He's frowning real hard now.

"I don't care how smart that bloody monster was; it didn't paint a sack with soot. I think someone's moved in here, Squirt. They must've figured on the dragon being dead even quicker than I did. Pretty risky call, but it looks like it's worked out for 'em, if they survived long enough to set this up. I bet they dumped that bit of coin in the first cave to distract anyone who might come along later, and then set this trap here in case that wasn't enough."

This is my chance. "So we go back, right? 'Cos it's not safe?"

"Nah, nah ..." Benji's still thinking. "Something doesn't add up. Why not just clean the place out and hide the money somewhere safer? I reckon we go check it out. Whoever it is can't be all that, or they wouldn't've bothered with the traps and distractions. I bet if you give 'em a bit of the old trollblood charm, they'll go running."

He grins at me. "There, see? And you thought I only brought you along to carry the bags."

He must see something in my face then, because he comes back and squeezes my shoulder again.

"Hey. Ellie. It's OK. I know we've had a fright, but we got through it, didn't we? We got through it 'cos you look out for me and I look out for you.

"So now we're just gonna go see what's what. We'd be fools not to at least have a look, right? But we'll go nice and careful, and we'll look out for each other, and if we see anything we can't handle, we'll get out of here. OK? You just say the word and we're gone."

He thinks he means it, too.

I want to say the word. There are so many words in my head, tumbling over each other. It doesn't matter. There's no word I could speak that would make him listen to me. Clever Benji always knows what's best.

My brother winks at me.

"Come on, Squirt. Let's go get rich."

***

We take it real slow after that. Benji keeps stopping to check all around us, but he doesn't find any more traps. Only wet rocks and darkness. My feet drag like they're made of lead, but I know it doesn't matter how slow we go. We're still going the wrong way.

And sure enough, after an age of walking and climbing and walking again, there's light ahead that doesn't come from our lamp. It's warm and yellow, like firelight, but it doesn't flicker like fire.

Benji puts out the lantern and we creep forward.

The tunnel opens up into a big cavern, the biggest we've seen. This is where the light comes from. It isn't firelight, though it's warm—not just warm yellow, but warm on our skins, like standing in the doorway to a cozy room.

It comes from the heap of gold in the middle of the floor.

I can believe this came from two temples and a bank. There's more money here than has passed through my hands and Benji's and everyone we've known our entire lives.

Benji looks at me, and his gold-lit face is grinning so wide it's almost split in two.

He's smart, though. He doesn't just go in, but stops and studies the whole place real careful.

The money's in a kind of bowl in the middle of the floor, and all around are rocks sticking up from the ground, but these aren't like the rocks in the other caves. These are carved. Ranks upon ranks of statues all over the place, like an army that doesn't know how to line up straight.

Some of the carvings are rough, but others are as fine as you'd see in front of a great lord's house. There are stone people, stone animals, and things that don't seem to know what to be. One rock close to me looks a bit like a bear, but then the way I'm looking at it shifts and it's more like a house. The gold-light runs down smooth faces and catches on tiny edges, making strange patterns of light and shadow that catch at my eyes.

There's no sign of any sculptor. The light doesn't quite reach all the way to the back of the cave, but there's no people anywhere we can see, and no sounds either. Benji takes another minute to look around, and then he steps out into the light and stands still, tense and ready to run.

Nothing happens.

Benji lets out an echoing whoop that makes me jump clear to the ceiling. "Look at this, Squirt! We're rich!" He grins at me again, all teeth, then turns and runs between the statues down into the cavern.

My heart's pounding fit to burst, but I follow.

The dragon-worn path makes a wide corridor between the carvings. The ground crunches underfoot and a forest smell rises up, sharp and clean, like pinecones thrown on a winter fire. There are pine needles scattered all over the floor here. The smell would be a comfort, if things were different.

Gold doesn't glow, of course. We reach the pile and there are eggs in it, a dozen or more, the exact same color as the coins they're nestled in. Each one is as big as my fist or Benji's head, and they're glowing from the inside. I look at the closest one and think I can see something inside it, against the light—a little form curled up and waiting.

Benji grabs the egg I was looking at and hefts it, feeling its weight. I freeze, watching it bounce. Does the shape inside shudder a little?

"Gods above, Ellie, Fortune is smiling on us today! That fool dragon went and died and left a clutch behind! We find the right buyer for these beauties, I reckon we could ask a thousand sovereigns for each one." He laughs a gleeful laugh.

My throat goes tight. There's an ache in my gut, growing harder and heavier by the second.

"Benji?" I say. "What if we just leave the eggs?" It comes out like a child's question, and I hate the sound of it.

"Oh for fuck's sake, Ellie! Now what?"

He glares at me, and there's real hurt behind his anger. All he sees in these eggs are gold rings and new dresses, and he honestly doesn't understand why I don't share in his delight. How can I make him understand?

I try one more time. "They're not ours to take."

"Not ours? What're you talking about, troll-skull? We found 'em! And they're gonna make us so rich you'll never have to kill another pig in your life! But you don't wanna take 'em?"

He turns his back on me and starts shoving gold and eggs into his rucksack, fast and angry.

"I swear, I don't know what goes on in your head these days. I thought we were a team, but here you are dragging your heels like a spoiled child every step of the way ..."

One of the eggs knocks against another as he shoves it in the sack. There's a noise like a tiny explosion, and then the light from the second egg fades away.

"Now look what you made me do," Benji snarls without looking up.

My breath stops.

Benji tosses the dark egg to one side. It lands with a sad crunching sound, and a thick, clear liquid starts to ooze out of it.

I look to the shadows down the far end of the cave, but I can't make out anything in the darkness there. The only sound, the only movement comes from Benji, all cursing and muttering and sharp-edged motion.

Fluid is pooling around the dark egg now, seeping away at angles where it catches on the pine needles.

I have to do something.

All around me, golden light glares off chiseled faces. A sharp-featured man stares at me, standing tall in robes and crown. A woman wearing a hawk's mask, or perhaps a bird with the arms of a woman, reaches out to me. Further back, a rough-hewn dragon, barely-defined in crude strokes simply watches.

It's up to me. I stand up tall, and I try to draw strength from the unmoving stone around me.

"Benji," I say, and my voice is not a child's. It is mine.

Benji ignores me, still scooping up gold and eggs.

"Benji," I say again, and when he still pays me no mind I step forward and take him by the shoulder and turn him to face me.

He yelps like a startled dog and tries to twist out of my grasp. I hold on tight, and try not to squeeze too hard. I'm being careful, but this is the first time in our lives I've laid a hand on him, and his eyes are wide. My hand engulfs his bony shoulder.

I look him right in the eyes, and the outrage there makes my heart jump up, but I swallow and say, "These eggs don't belong to us, Benji. They're living things, and they got just as much a right to live as we do. You wanted gold, and you got it, more than we can ever use. Let's just take what we can carry and go."

I say it firm, standing up strong like stone, even though my guts are twisting and there's a part of me that's trying to curl up and hide.

Benji's mouth is open, but no sound comes out. I open my hand, and he bounces away from it like it's a punch, cradling his arm to his chest.

Is he hurt? I need to tell him I didn't mean to hurt him. He needs to know I didn't want to do it this way. I only wanted him to listen to me, really listen for once.

"Benji—" I say.

That's as far as I get before he starts laughing. It's a hard, angry laugh, sharp-edged like a broken mirror.

"What the fuck was that, troll-skull? You think 'cos you've got muscles for brains I'm gonna start taking orders from you now? Well sure, why not! You can be in charge! I'll just stay home and let you look after me, since you've clearly got it all figured out. Don't worry about paying rent, you can just flex your muscles at Old Man Tally till he lets us stay for free. And when we get hungry you can just punch us up some food!"

"I just want you to listen-"

"Listen to what?" he snaps, and there's no laughter in him now.

"Some half-baked ideas about *ooooh, all life is sacred?* Fuck that. No one thought our lives were sacred when we were cold and alone on the streets. No one thought *your* miserable trollblood life was worth saving except for *me*, remember? And now you're worrying about a pack of monsters just like the one that got our idiot dad killed? If you want me to listen to you, troll-skull, then stop talking such shit. Until then, stick to what you're good at."

He turns away from me, grabbing for the half-filled rucksack with its precious cargo. There's a pressure in my skull that I don't know what to do with. Words, words, words. No matter what I say, Benji will always twist it around to serve him. Words are his weapon.

So I stick to what I'm good at.

Benji squawks and drops the bag as I lift him up, as easy as lifting a child, and pin him against the nearest statue. It's a tree, gnarled and ancient but barely taller than me, the egg-light turning its leaves to autumn. Benji shouts at me, and struggles and kicks, but I use my weight to hold him still, pressing the breath out of him when he tries to squeal, like I learned in The Shambles. He weighs so much less than a pig.

There's a moment, then, like a pitcher teetering on the edge of a table. I'm looking down at us from somewhere overhead—the hulking trollblood crushing the life out of this fragile stick of a man—and I can see how easy it would be for the monster to push a little harder, for the vessel to tip and shatter. And then I'm looking into my brother's eyes, and the horror of what I'm doing climbs up my throat and tries to choke me.

"Enough," I tell him. My voice comes out a growl I don't recognize. "We're not taking the eggs, Benji. Leave them alone and go. Get out of here."

I give him one last squeeze for emphasis, and then I step back and lower him gently to the ground.

He's gasping for breath, spitting filth at me with all the wind he has, but the hard edge is missing from his voice. And then there's the way he's looking at me.

I don't even step towards him, just shift my weight, and he flinches.

"Benji—"

"Screw you," he gasps, hopping from foot to foot. "Screw you, troll-skull. Let's see how you like being the big troll when you're out there all on your own. Fuck it. I'm done with you."

His eyes twitch towards his rucksack, but I'm standing between him and it, and there are still eggs inside. Then he's off and running, back up the worn path, disappearing into the dark and taking our only lantern with him.

My legs don't want to hold me anymore, so I sit down hard on the uneven floor, crunching up the pine needles. In the golden egg-light, stone faces gaze down at me. A solemn fish-tailed man. A long, pointed muzzle that might belong to a horse, or perhaps a serpent.

There's no water here to drip. The silence of this place is so big it's almost a sound, pressing in against my ears. An endless darkness of sound.

And then there's a noise so faint it's barely there, and the shadow at the far end of the cave unfolds, and the dragon drops down to the floor.

Benji was wrong. She's not dead. But she's old, so old. Her copper-dark scales are rough and time-scored. They're starting to glow, now that she's done hiding, but their light is faded and dull, just like her great round eyes. Her head wobbles on her long, thin neck, and the skin of her wings drags on the ground as she shuffles towards the gold.

I sit very still.

The dragon circles the pile until she finds Benji's rucksack and sniffs at it. With a claw she teases it open. Gently, she begins replacing the eggs and the gold in her nest. Her hands are even bigger than mine, and they shake a little with age, but her touch is as delicate as an artist's as she positions each egg, each coin, exactly where it's meant to be.

She looks so tired these days.

The first time I saw her, she was bigger, less folded in on herself. Her eyes were already filmy, but her neck arched and her gaze was sharp enough to pin me in place. Her wings, when she stretched them out, reflected the light from her scales and glowed like paper lanterns.

She was so beautiful then. And there I was covered in pig's blood from a bucket, snot running down my face.

I'd run away to escape the laughter of the butchers' boys, to escape the stares and the curses and the shame. I had run all the way to the caves, to where our dad died, looking for the monster that killed him. Looking for escape.

I found it. But not how I meant it.

When everything is back in its right place, the dragon shuffles over to me. I stand up, and she drapes her neck over my shoulder. She thrums low, and it rumbles through my bones as: Thank you.

I've been keeping my thoughts far away, but that brings me right back to here and the tears start running down my face.

"I'm sorry," I whisper into her neck. The broken egg sits dark at our feet. "I'm sorry. I should've been stronger, I should've done something sooner ..."

She hums words I don't know, but the sound is soothing. I lean into her scratchy scales, closing my eyes and taking comfort from her fading warmth. In the dark, if I let my head go empty, I can almost pretend it's just another day, and I've come down here to see her, to learn from her, and to hide away from the world for a while.

She only knows a little of my speech and I know none of hers, but neither of us is much for talking anyway. I bring her stolen meat and pine needles to make the cave smell nice, and she lets me use her tools: hammers and chisels of a hard, heavy metal, all of a piece like they were poured into shape, and files made from her own shed skin. She teaches me how to read the stone and find the forms hidden inside, how to carve them into life.

Even without language, her patience is endless. My sculptures aren't as good as hers yet, but I'm getting close. Turns out my hands are fine for delicate work, with the right tools and the right teacher.

Past her shoulder, half-hidden by the horse that might be a serpent, two stone figures—one tall, one short—clasp hands.

Benji doesn't mean it, I think, not even after what I did. He'll go home, and then he'll wait for me. He'll wait until I've been lost and alone in the dark long enough that I'll run home and tell him I'm sorry and I'll never do it again and beg him to please just take care of me.

There's a part of me that wishes I could still run home to him. But I saw the way he looked at me, the same way people at the market have always looked at me, even though I've never laid a finger on anyone before.

I wanted things to change, but not like this.

What will he do, when I don't come home? Will he forget about me and get on with his life?

Or will he come back with friends? Big friends, with blades and cudgels? I don't think he would want to hurt me. But I do think he wants the riches here enough that he might overlook what his friends are willing to do to help him get them. He might even think it's for my own good. A reminder of why I should let him do the thinking. He only wants to look out for me.

"There's something I have to do," I say, and though I doubt the dragon knows the words, I think she understands. I take one of the lanterns I stashed away here, and the biggest of the hammers and chisels, and go back into the dark.

***

There's a few spots of green painting the walls of the entrance chamber, the glow-bugs still unsure but coming back to life. The decoy gold is piled up where we left it. I leave it there—if Benji does come back, at least he'll have that. We have to look out for each other.

It's narrowest here, in the tunnel I had to lift him up to reach, barely wide enough for a dragon to squeeze through. I raise up the lantern and read the stone, just like I've been taught. I tap the ceiling with the butt of a chisel and let it speak to me, here and here and ...there.

I swing the hammer in the cramped space and drive the point of the chisel into the ceiling. I beat on it until it's wedged in tight, and the crack that was hidden inside the stone has opened up and is worming its way across the ceiling, and then I take another chisel and begin again.

Again and again I swing my hammer, driving metal into stone. The impacts shudder through my body like sorrow, like rage, like the two fused together into something too big for me to name.

Stupid Ellie, trying to stand up for herself, proving herself the monster everyone's always known she was. Stupid Benji, treating me like a child, forcing me to be the monster I never wanted to be.

I hammer, and I howl, and the stone howls back at me as the ceiling comes crashing down. I cover my eyes and choke and cough, and when the dust settles the tunnel is gone, just a wall of rubble, and tears are running down my cheeks again.

It's not the only way into the cave system. The dragon has shown me others that come out in the forest on the other side of the hills. But only she and I, and perhaps some forest animals, know about those ones. As far as Abercoombe will see, the cave is gone—all its secrets sealed away in the dark.

There's wetness dribbling down my face. I reach up and tighten the bandage around my head, feeling the ragged edges of Benji's torn shirt soft against my fingers.

When I get back to the big cave, the dragon is singing.

She's crouched beside her nest, holding the cracked egg in her hands. The sound she's making is so low I can feel it more than hear it. I'm not sure if there are words in it. It's hard to tell with dragon-speech, but I don't think so. Only sorrow and love so deep I could drown in them.

I sit with my back against a miniature stone cathedral, breathing in dragon-song. Tears blur my sight, and I'm not even sure who I'm crying for anymore, the dragon or me or Benji or all of us together.

Stone figures gaze down on me without judgment. The dragon extends a ragged wing, and I crawl across the floor to sit beneath it. Under my knees, the scent rises of pinecones on a winter fire.

Through my tears, the rest of the eggs glow like church windows. The shapes inside are moving, swaying to their mother's song. They barely fit in their shells anymore. Soon they will hatch.

Good. I can scrounge up enough food for the old dragon and me, while we wait. I can find the life in the last of these stones and use hammer and chisel and file to give it shape.

The old dragon might live to see it or she might not, but they will hatch, these beautiful monsters, big-eyed and golden-winged, and maybe they will live with the stone-folk in the caves under Abercoombe, but I think they will leave here and go out into the world, and see what lies beyond.

I think I will too.

A Song For Hardy Connelly

K. Noel Moore

K. Noel Moore's fiction appears in briars lit, Teleport, X-R-A-Y, and Vulture Bones, as well as on Kindle, where she has published one novella (a ghost drama entitled Undertown) and has another in the works. You can find her tweeting @mysterioustales or blogging at theoutlawwrites.tumblr.com.

This story is dedicated to Kelly Moore-Campbell: beloved aunt, leader, and inspiration, more whole than whole. *Ar scáth a chéile a mhaireann na daoine.*

I. Hardy

According to Moïra, it was after the loss of her parents to the Connelly curse that she stopped believing in Mass, and started believing in magic.

My aunt Moïra disdained ceremony and lived for festivity. She drank too much, lived too hard, and blamed it on the blood in her veins. In appearance, she was the opposite of her brother, who was my father: a big, muscled woman, with a head of unruly dark curls, and thick tangles of Celtic tattoos on her arms. She wore good-luck charms around her neck and prayed to gods who'd been mostly forgotten long ago.

The first time I met Moïra, I was eleven, stuck in the hospital as doctors ran their battery of tests to discover why my legs no longer held my weight. Mother and Father had both worn themselves out waiting by my bedside, and I knew they would have to go home in time—but I was surprised at who came to replace them. Not a grandmother. Not a teenage cousin. A perfect stranger, dressed in motorcycle gear.

The woman brushed raindrops from her clothes and ran a hand through her hair, pulling the staticky mess of it under some control. Her chapped, cut lips formed words, directed at my mother. I didn't and still don't read lips easily or well, but I managed to make out the words *"wouldn't," "options," "rest,"* and *"thank you,"* before Mother sighed in resignation. She then signed to me, explaining that this stranger was Father's sister, Moïra, and that she would be taking care of me for a day or two.

Father's sister Moïra waved to me in greeting, and I saw scrapes on her knuckles and black paint on her nails.

We made conversation in careful, halting Sign; what words she didn't know, we wrote in bright purple on the little white-board I used to communicate with the doctors. She translated her conversation with my parents: they "wouldn't have imposed if they had any other option," but they "just needed a rest for tonight." (Meaning, she said, that she and my mother weren't on good terms, but she was desperate for a break and no one else had offered to come and sit with me.) I told her about the hospital, asked her what riding a motorcycle was like, complained about Father and Mother pressuring me to wear uncomfortable hearing-aids to *"make things easier on them."* She sympathized with my annoyance with "Alfie," as she called him, and told me he'd been the way he was since he was a little boy.

Then I asked her why I'd never met her. In fact, before that night, I'd had only a vague idea that Father *had* a younger sister.

She considered the question for a moment. Finally, she signed to me, 'Ghost stories like you?'

I didn't understand the change of subject, but I nodded. 'All stories I like.'

Moïra smiled, showing all her teeth. She always showed all her teeth when she smiled. 'I tell you story, want you?'

My nodding then was even more eager. I all but forgot about the question I'd asked. I was bored out of my skull, and it wasn't even close to the time I usually fell asleep; a story to occupy my mind would be an oasis in the desert. Moïra picked up the marker. 'Your parents don't want me to tell you any of this,' she wrote, 'but I think it's time you knew.'

'Story true?'

'Yes.'

Moïra told me everything that night.

She told me that the gold of my eyes, the faint sheen behind light brown that drew what attention could be pulled away from my talking hands and failing legs was the telltale sign of the second sight. *Second sight*, she told me, was what let us see places where the Other Place bled into our own world. Moïra's eyes had the same gold in them.

'Other Place, what?'

'The world beyond. Where things that aren't human live.'

That made me shiver.

She told me that sometime during the Age of Empire, though so muddled by time and deliberate attempts to hide the truth that no one remembers the exact year, the Ó Conghalaighs of the old country had meddled with something from the Other Place that wasn't meant to be meddled with, which was why their blood-line was cursed with hardship—often with early death. She told me our history. She told me of the Connelly ghost, the spirit of a woman in burned clothing, whose weird musical keening heralded misfortune. 'Those of us with the second sight can see her face-to-face, or hear her singing outside our windows.' She erased, kept writing. 'Those without it see her, or hear her, or both, in their dreams.'

A delicious shudder ran up my spine. 'Deaf I,' I signed, smiling. 'Not hear ghost.' I didn't mention that, sometimes, I detected something like sound in my dreams, something that seemed to come straight into my mind. I wondered if it was Moïra's "Other Place," reaching out to me.

'True. You have.' She paused. 'A-D-V-A-N-T-A-G-E.'

'Why parents no want me know this?'

'Your parents want forget past. I think should remember. They try forget me.'

The thought of being forgotten scared me worse than any of the ghosts she'd told me of, worse than any strange thing my golden eyes had already showed me. I tried to pull my legs against my chest, only to remember it was useless.

Moïra patted my knee, comforting me. 'Strong you,' she signed, and then, as if correcting herself, 'Strong we. Different we. Survive we.'

Moïra left the next morning. I wouldn't see her again until I was thirteen.

The braces around my legs clunked and clanged as I climbed the creaky stairs to Moïra's front door. Her house, with its slanted roof and its faded paint, looked like it belonged in a black-and-white photo, which, according to what Mother told me, it did; the house had been in our family since the thirties, as long as our blood had been in America.

"Do you need help, Hardy?" Mother asked, her concerned eyes locked onto my legs. Her words were fuzzy and faint.

I shook my head. "I can make it."

"Are you sure?"

"Yes, Mother."

Still, she stared.

Since I went into remission, it seemed like people couldn't help but stare at me. Well, they stared at the metal parts of me, anyway: the braces around my legs, the machines in my ears. They whispered behind their hands, thinking that just because I couldn't hear, I wouldn't know. They forgot that the Deaf know the language of expression and gesture better than anybody.

Poor thing, they said. *Cursed she must be. That's no worthwhile life she's living.*

I could have interrupted. I could have explained to them, in scholarly terms that would have left them staring in surprise instead of pity, about childhood Guillain-Barré Syndrome and various reasons I may have been born Deaf. I could tell them every good reason my life *was* worth living. Instead, I pretended I didn't notice. It's always easier, I find, to let people continue believing whatever they believed before.

Mother rang the doorbell, and was answered with a shout from inside, "It's open!" She shooed me inside like a cat, before stepping inside herself, hauling both of our overnight bags.

Moïra was, as mother liked to say, "in a bad way." ("In a bad way" was her catch-all euphemism for the things she wanted to keep from me, that bad family fortune.) Being "in a bad way" didn't stop Moïra from being her bustling self, however. When we entered the house, we found her standing in the foyer, using the coatrack as a wobbly crutch. She was grinning.

"Good Lord, Moïra," Mother scolded her, "you shouldn't be up. In fact," she muttered, "you shouldn't be out of the hospital at all."

"I don't believe in hospitals." With a quick glance at me, she added, "Not as applies to me, I mean. Doctors have their place. But when it's my time, I'd rather be in my own home. Not in some lifeless hulking thing crammed with suffering folks. Not being prodded and dissected by a bunch of strangers."

"'Your time.' Goodness. You talk as if you're dying—which, right *now*, you aren't, but you'll end up killing yourself if you carry on like this. Go sit down, before you trip on a stair and break your neck."

Moïra's legs were so heavily bandaged that she could barely move them at all, only stiffly and slowly, and I noticed she gritted her teeth when she did. Two of her fingers were splinted, and she had an ugly purple-green bruise on her forehead. 'Bike crash,' she signed to me when she caught me staring.

I nodded. 'Mother tell me.'

Mother gave us both a hard look that said *shush*. I shoved my hands into my pockets.

Moïra pulled a face at Mother. I'd never seen an adult "pulling a face"—which was another of Mother's favorite phrases— at another adult, but that's exactly what she did. "Let the girl talk, Alice."

"If Hardy wants to talk," Mother replied, "she can use her *words*."

For a second, Moïra's look could have killed; then, it twisted into a smirk. "*Abair arís é go mall, le do thoil?*"

Her retort sounded so strange to my ears, I thought my hearing-aids had broken. I took one out and shook it, before I realized she wasn't speaking English.

Mother's face crinkled in confusion. *"What?"*

I put my hearing-aid back in just in time to hear Moïra's reply. "Oh, I'm sorry, I thought you wanted us speaking our second languages. Well, to be fair, I've tried to pick up a language plenty of times over the years, never really had the patience for it." She looked down at her bandaged legs. "I'll be out of commission for a while, though, so I'll have time to brush up on my Gaelige. Maybe this time it'll stick."

I repeated the unfamiliar word, *Gaelige*, aloud, and she spelled it for me with her hands. "Irish," she said aloud, and then, to me: 'How sign I-R-I-S-H?'

I showed her, creating the word in the standard thing that is form, as in, *American—America-thing that is*. Or *bad luck-thing that is*—the closest thing Sign has to a word for *cursed*. *Ireland-thing that is—Irish*. She nodded, copying my motions.

"What did you take that up for?" Mother interrupted. "There's no practical use for that, not that I can see."

"Tír gan teanga, tír gan anam." She shrugged as well as she could while still holding herself up. "The past informs the present, those who forget their history are doomed to repeat it, et cetera, et cetera."

"Those who forget their history...yes, I understand that," Mother said. "But then there's those who forget that they live in the present. Who cling to fantasies of something they never lived."

Moïra's usual easygoing smirk faded, replaced by thin lips and chilly silence.

Mother shot another sharp glance at me. For all she pushed me to hear, it seemed like she wanted me Deaf when it was convenient for her.

"Go rest," she told Moïra, sighing her most Motherly *whatever will I do with this child* sigh. "Alfie will be here tomorrow, he'll know how best to get you back on your feet." Brooking no argument, she put an arm around her waist and helped her to an old leather couch in the living room. "I'll start dinner. Keep an eye on Hardy, please, as best you can without getting up. And *don't* tell her any more of your ridiculous stories!"

I took my hearing-aids out as soon Mother was gone from the room. 'Thank you,' I signed. 'For stand up to Mother.'

'Family you,' she replied. 'Good family protect each other.' Her Sign was much more confident and quick than it had been, I noticed, and she noticed my noticing. 'I lie her. For one thing I have patience. I have patience learn Sign.'

I thanked her again. 'More stories you tell me?'

She feigned shock. 'Your mother say no! Break rule we!'

'I not mind,' I signed, with all the eagerness to mischief of every child that age.

Moïra sat back a moment, thinking. 'No more stories have I,' she finally replied. 'I tell you all. Maybe you tell me story now.'

'Me'—my face froze. I wasn't sure what to express, puzzlement or shock or flattery.

She nodded yes. 'Family history I write,' she told me. 'History of people with....' She paused, at a loss for a sign, and finally she pointed to her eye. I understood. 'Your story I need. You write for me maybe.'

The idea of my story standing among a proud lineage—the idea of no longer being alone in the weird visions I glimpsed from the corner of my eye—thrilled me. I went into her study, rifled through the desk for cheap stationery, and when I had some in hand, I sat beside her on the sofa and began to write, unaware that the story I wove was about to gain a new chapter.

I dreamt of sound, and woke to soundlessness.

Unsure what had woken me, I rolled off the large chair I'd fallen asleep on, shrugging off the knit blanket Mother had wrapped around me. (Mother had taken the bedroom for herself; the closet wouldn't close, and it made me nervous, especially with Moïra's insistence that something lived in there.) I looked around; Moïra also wasn't where she had fallen asleep.

Fingers brushed my shoulder, and I jumped. It was her, of course. She was supporting her weight on the windowsill; if not for the gloriously bright moon, I wouldn't have seen the motion of her hands. 'Come,' she signed. 'Look.'

The spirit that moved, barely visible, through the yard, drifting close to the window, Moïra had called a B-E-A-N-S-I-D-H-E, though she had explained to me back when I was eleven that she wasn't certain it was one in a traditional sense; beansidhes were said to appear at the time of a death, and this ghostly woman heralded more general misfortune. She appeared younger than Moïra, but with a look of long, hard years in her eyes. Her dress was centuries out of style, covered in soot and tattered. Her hair was the same dark red as mine, wild and messy. Her face was soot-streaked as well, tracked with long-shed tears. Her mouth was open, to scream or to speak or to sing a piercing note, I couldn't tell.

Then, my attention shifted from her, to the trees behind her. They weren't our trees, I knew it. *The Other Place*, I thought, my breath catching in my throat. From where this woman had come, or how she would return, or if I could reach that place myself, I didn't know, but I was sure of what I saw. My second sight had finally showed me, in full, what existed beyond our world.

Moïra's eyes burned gold in the ghostly light, and I wondered if she thought the same thing I did.

Home.

II. Saraid

Us Ò Conghalaighs have witchery in our blood.

magic in the hills. charms about necks and offerings under trees, altars in homes and icons over fireplaces. folk come to us for luck, for health, for love. English soldiers staring in the streets. my brother spits at them. "éire inniu éire amárach éire go brách"

"golden-eyes," they call us. disdain and fear. "enchanters."

all but little Saraid. little Saraid, with no gifts. with no witchery. no gold in her eyes. no sight in her eyes.

Us Ò Conghalaighs have darkness in our blood.

they have sought something dark. and they have found it. there are things in the Other Place that shouldn't be touched, and my sisters and brothers have taken them in both hands.

only dark magic comes from want of power. only bad magic is used for revenge.

the Ò Conghalaigh enchanters let the darkness in. little Saraid, with no gold in her eyes, pays the price.

"tine! tine istigh cillín!

fire! fire in the church!"

Us Ò Conghalaighs—aren't Ò Conghalaighs any longer, and with the way time flows like honey in the Other Place, I have to remind myself of it all the time.

Us *Connellys* have a curse on our blood.

Deaths. Accidents. Illnesses. Fires like the one that took me. Centuries, and an ocean, haven't stopped the incidents, and at each one, I find myself compelled to sing, to mourn.

Inniu. Amárach. Go brách. Today, tomorrow, forever. You can cross an ocean, you can change a name, you can forget the old country, but the old country never forgets you. The hills do not forget. The Other Place does not forget.

Who knew that little blind Saraid, with no gold in her eyes, was the one who belonged among shades and daemons?

III. Moïra

Another funeral. Only time all us Connellys ever saw each other, and considering how small the cluster of towns is where we all made our dwellings, it took effort never to see each other.

I heard the song again the night before, and for the first time since my accident, my fatigue overwhelmed my desire to go after it. Maybe Alfie and Alice were right all along, I thought. Maybe the way to make this thing die off is just to pretend it doesn't exist. Shut our eyes and cover our ears and hide under our blankets waiting for the monsters to pass.

I leaned heavily on my cane, twisting the charm around my neck as I glanced nervously around the crowd. Some days I still wasn't used to walking with a limp. Some days I forgot the new Moïra Connelly altogether, and went about my morning forgetting I needed a steadying agent, until I stumbled into my kitchen counter. That morning had been one of those. My hip still ached from the bruise I'd acquired.

From the grove beyond the graveyard, over the droning of many voices, I heard the creak of a rusty swing. Curious, I followed the sound, out of the land of carefully-shorn grass and plastic flowers into wild trees.

The swings were covered in moss—along with a few broken birdbaths, and cobblestones poking out from beneath the leaves under my feet, they were the remnants of a long-forgotten garden. The creaking was made by a young woman, swinging slowly back and forth. Red-haired, grey-and-gold-eyed. Braces on her legs. I knocked on the swing-set with my cane, prompting her to look up, and tapped my hand—shaped in the Sign letter H—against my chest.

She made a similar gesture, her hand forming a letter M: 'Moïra.'

I sat down on the other swing and kicked my legs, happy to see they were still useful for something. 'Why you here?' I signed.

'No like people stare.'

I nodded my agreement. 'I no like either.' I used the tip of my cane to indicate her braces. 'Same we now.'

'Same we,' she echoed.

'How old you now?'

'Seventeen.'

'Seventeen! Almost grown you. Old I.'

'Old you no!' she signed, and laughed. It occurred to me that, whether we realize it or not, all of us that can hear will at some point feel insecure about our voices, our laughs. Hardy had no such insecurity, and it was a beautiful thing.

She shot my query back at me: 'Why you here?'

I shrugged. 'No believe in church,' I signed with a flippant expression. Then, I grew sober. 'I no want talk to family. Family not want talk to me either. Black sheep I.'

Again, she signed: 'Same we.' Then: 'What this place?'

'Garden,' I answered, punctuating it with another shrug. 'Old place.' I wracked my brain for the sign for "ruin"—the place *was* a ruin, I thought, and a truly beautiful one, like a half-smashed Aztec pyramid without all the tourists—but couldn't find it. Once there was something beautiful here.

'Ruin,' Hardy signed. An X sliding forward and curling up over another X.

I nodded. 'Yes, exactly. Ruin. Beautiful,' I added.

Hardy edged off the swing, the closest thing she could manage to jumping. 'You want know why I here?' She didn't give me a chance to nod. 'I find,' she signed, beaming expectantly at me.

'You find what?'

'Door.'

My arms pricked with goosebumps. The door. Since Hardy was thirteen, we had emailed back and forth near-constantly, we had spoken of finding a "door" to the Other Place, somewhere the worlds bled together so much that we might find ourselves walking beyond.

Hardy believed it was here. In this garden. Could it really be so? All this time, had it been mere walking distance from the little Irish Catholic church where I'd sat every Sunday as a child?

She hesitated, then slowly and carefully Signed, 'I go. You want go with me?'

My throat dry and my heart hammering, I nodded yes. 'Yes, of course, yes.' The apathy of the previous night was gone; the drive in me to find the Other Place had never been stronger.

She took my hand, which surprised me at first, but I understood a moment later: she wanted our journey to be silent. She wanted me to privately take it all in and let her do the same.

I breathed in, holding the air of this world in my lungs one final time, and I followed her.

I remember what I told her that night in the hospital. *We are different. We survive.*

I remember sleeping fitfully on a row of plastic chairs shoved together. Waiting for the sound. Hardy's song. I remember it never came. I remember Alfie telling me he waited the same way, in the hospital when she was sick and in the hospital when she was born, when he was told she would never hear, and it never came. The song of Connelly tragedy never came for Hardy. No, there's another song for her: the flute music of the Other Place.

I don't know where she's leading me. I don't know what we'll find on the other side of the door, if we find the door at all. I don't know what awaits us, if time will start again, or if it will move like honey the way it does in the Other Place, or if we'll remain in this moment forever. I don't know what awaits the blood we left on the other side.

I know nothing, but still I follow Hardy.

Because I know one thing: we are different. We survive. We are golden-eyes, we are broken and we are more whole than whole, we are the last Ò Conghalaighs of the hills.

We belong among the shades and daemons.

Auger

Sarah Pauling

Sarah's work is published or upcoming in Strange Horizons, Cast of Wonders, and Abyss & Apex. If approached without sudden movement, she can be found at @_paulings on Twitter, where she natters on about writing, tabletop gaming, comics, and books.

A long seashell rests on the mermaid's breastbone, dangling from the rope of algae slime around her neck. The shell is delicately off-white and scuffed with brown, spiraling into a tapered end that points to the water's surface.

Henrik stares; remembers last summer's long days by the harbor collecting sharp auger shells like this one to have sword fights with his brother. Pretending they were knives.

The mermaid submerges the rest of her body in the freezing water of the little inlet: straight down, no splash, until all that remains are her black eyes, her pallid forehead, and her iridescent hair spreading like oil rainbows in water.

"So you can't tell anyone, alright?" Bartram tells Henrik and Inga nervously, pulling his shirt on over his wet, goosebumped skin. Henrik had watched him swish around in the freezing shallows for nearly fifteen minutes. He'd dangled Mama's whalebone bodkin needle into the water on a string until the mermaid recognized him by this strange sign and came to the surface. "Mama and Pa wouldn't like it."

"Why?" Henrik asks. "It's just a mermaid. Mermaids aren't bad."

Bartram squints at him, a mixture of nearsightedness and

big-brotherly frustration. "I don't know," he says, annoyed. "They just wouldn't like it." He sits down on the dock and rubs his arms.

"She's beautiful," Inga says wistfully, tucking disorganized curls behind her ears. Her bun is half-dismantled, allowing sea winds to tie her hair into knots. "I'm sure your parents wouldn't mind, would they? Or mine, either. I mean, my mama used to tell stories—"

A splash from the mermaid draws their attention. She bobs along with the gentle waves coming off the Øresund into the narrow, cliff-lined inlet near the city's harbor.

Her sparkling eyes are twice the size of a human's and entirely made up of pupil. Her skin has a sickly tinge to it: thin and papery but spiking with fever beneath. In the open air her hair looks like the inside of an uncleaned seashell: pink-white and slimy. When she reaches up to grasp the edge of the dock, her hands are disproportionately long and spidery, culminating in harpoon-sharp nails. She wears seaweed tangled between her fingers.

"Oh! I brought blackcurrants," Bartram tells her eagerly, reaching into his satchel. "I'll toss 'em to you again, if you want. Like a game."

She pushes away from the dock. Her smile, warm and genuine, has many teeth.

The children toss the berries. She catches most of them in her mouth with uncanny accuracy, but Bartram laughs hardest when the berries smack her in the face.

Her giggle comes soundless except for a faint wheezing and the fluttering of her gills.

She shows off by performing a sort of backwards dolphin leap, her scaled legs framed in spray and glistening.

Henrik decides he likes being friends with a mermaid. He isn't sure who wouldn't.

(At night he dreams of a fish unfurling itself by the scales then falling to pieces, like a long potato peel split in half by a knife.)

**

"Bartram and Inga and me made friends with a mermaid over by the bastion fort," he tells their parents during supper.

"*Henrik*," Bartram hisses through his teeth.

"Oh," Mama says. "Well fancy that!"

Pa frowns. "How do you know it's not a siren?"

"She's *not* a siren," Bartram says, stabbing at his herring. "She's definitely a mermaid." He glances murderously at Henrik.

"How do you tell the difference?" Mama asks Pa. "One of your shipmates saw a siren once, didn't he? Wasn't it—I think it was Tall Anders."

"It was Young Anders," Pa grumbles, "and he *thinks* he saw one as he was bent over a crate losing his mead. We were becalmed for one day and he lost his wits."

"Sirens are evil," Bartram says stubbornly. "She's not evil."

"That's right," Henrik says, feeling he ought to give his input. "She's nice and kind of shy."

"Eat your fish, Henrik," Mama says.

"The difference," Pa says with aplomb, "is the singing."

"I thought they both sang," Mama says. "It's just that mermaids sing about going to heaven, and sirens sing about—well, you know."

"No," Pa maintains. "No, sirens are the ones that sing. You be careful," he says, shooting a look at Bartram. "If it starts singing, plug up your ears and scoot. Sirens know how unstoppable a red-blooded man can get with a pretty woman in front of him. Never get into the water with it."

Bartram blushes. Mama says, "*Olaf!*"

"What? Cut me some slack, Hanne, you know it's true! That's just how boys are. It's healthy, s'long as it's not an evil fish you're chasing after. Now if it was that Inga girl he was fishing for—"

"Olaf—"

"I don't want to hear it," he says, holding up a hand in Mama's face. She sighs and spreads more butter on her potato.

Bartram's lips twist downwards. "She's *not* a siren. May I be excused? I'm not hungry anymore."

"For pity's sake, boy, you're fourteen," Pa says, a storm gathering on his features. "You'll need to eat more than that if you're going to come with me on the ship next year."

Bartram twirls his fork, eyes glued to his plate.

***

The grove of cherry trees by the bastion fort is maintained by the Crown, though Henrik has never seen the Crown do any gardening. On a chill morning, heavy mists cling to the grass between the trees, low and furtive like hiding ghosts.

Henrik spends hours by the dock watching the mermaid chase petals in the water when they drop down the rocky cliff into the inlet. Sometimes, with an odd shyness, she reaches up to hold his hand.

***

Inga grabs a fistful of the mermaid's hair.

The mermaid rears back with a terrible animal noise: a fleeing cat or a diving hawk. Her body jerks violently as she yanks at her own locks—as though she'd rather tear them to pieces in a tug-of-war with Inga than let her keep hold.

Inga lets go, shocked, and the mermaid tumbles into the water.

Henrik sees a flash of scales beneath the water, then nothing. The three children stand in silence on the dock. The sea roars from a distance.

"I'm sorry," Inga finally says, tears in her voice. She's barefoot, smock hanging loosely around her calves. "I just—I've wanted all day to tell her how pretty her hair is, and she wears it down like I've always wanted to, so I couldn't help myself, and just today Bartram said he pulls on mine because it's always coming loose and he can't help it—"

Bartram pats her back awkwardly.

"I couldn't help it," Inga says.

She pulls away from Bartram—and for a strange moment, she faces resistance. He grabs at the crook of her elbow.

Bartram's arms are slender and girlish. Pa says he'll look ridiculous holding a woman until he starts eating more red meat.

Bartram may look ridiculous, but he doesn't look powerless. His Adam's apple, increasingly prominent, bobs when he swallows. Henrik's caught him poking at it in the mirror, a wary expression on his face.

Inga and Bartram watch each other like they're not sure what should happen next. Then Inga wrenches harder until she's free.

"Don't you understand? I have to say I'm sorry, somehow."

Henrik watches the eddies slide back from the shore, cannibalizing the arriving swell.

"I couldn't *help* it," Inga says.

Angry nail marks dot her arm like pitted wood.

***

That night, Bartram wakes his little brother up with a choked-off scream. He bites down on his pillow until he calms down. It wouldn't do to let Pa hear him thrashing off a nightmare.

Henrik sits in the darkness for a long time, hardly daring to move. His brother's arm goes limp against his.

Bartram whispers his dream aloud: his own fingers but strong, stronger than a thousand heaving sailors—his own hands crushing sand into pearls.

***

Four days later, the mermaid retches like a cat. She spits up a piece of amber.

Bartram looks askance at the lopsided rock as it rolls down the dock, but Henrik understands the peace offering right away: Inga wears an amber necklace. She never takes it off.

The mermaid's amber is unpolished, its clouded edges worn down by the sea. Inga doesn't seem to care. She beams as she pockets it. Rather than crowd the mermaid, she hugs Bartram so tightly he turns red.

The amber keeps a bug trapped inside: a many-legged smudge, dark and broken.

***

"I can't stay for long," Bartram says, rubbing his arms against the evening chill. "Pa wants me to come with him on deck tomorrow—learn about lines."

"What *about* them?" Henrik asks. He leans back against the church wall, eyes on the path to the mermaid-dock.

"What? I dunno," Bartram says, kicking at an unbloomed daffodil. "It's—you know, lines. For heaving. Trimming sails. Cabin boy stuff."

"Maybe Inga would like you more if you knew about lines."

"Shut up," Bartram scowls. "Really, shut up."

Then Bartram is quiet for awhile. The gloom casts shadows beneath his sunken eyes as the church tolls out the quarter-hour. He hasn't been sleeping much. When he does, he talks to ghosts.

"Bartram?"

"I told Inga how I feel about her," Bartram says. The wind picks up, tossing through his hair. His dark irises look nearly black.

"You asked her to *marry* you?"

"No! I mean, not yet. But...I *knew* she won't give me a proper chance." He rubs his arms rhythmically, self-soothingly. "And—and it's not fair, because she *should* like me. We have so much—we have everything in common! And it's not like I *can't* do all that other stuff. The sailing stuff, and the wood chopping and the eating eggs to get strong, and the—with girls—"

"She's ready!" Inga says, marching up the path. Her moonlit forehead sparkles with sweat from the brief hike down to the inlet. Henrik hears Bartram swallow down a lump in his throat.

Beside her, the mermaid walks.

She wears an old dress belonging to Inga's mother, patterned in tulips with a trim of lace around the collar. The cloth, tight in the arms but loose in the chest, seems to come together for the purpose of suffocating her at the neck.

She stands a head taller than even Inga, who guides her by the elbow. The mermaid's toes curl into the grass like she's putting down roots; her posture suggests clumsiness or even dizziness.

Her yellowed smile is confident and lovely.

The church chimes the half hour.

The mermaid turns to Henrik—reaches out for him, calls him. Each witch-sharp fingernail curves inwards, one by one in a gentle wave, coming to rest at the heel of her palm.

Come.

Henrik tells the mermaid: "You got something green in your teeth," and takes her hand.

They walk with fingers interlaced. The mermaid is careful, and Henrik is not cut.

***

Dirty pink petals litter the grass of the cherry grove. The trees are nearly naked now. Soon green leaves will replace the burst of surreal color as the fallen petals are shredded and trampled into the earth.

The friends sprawl beneath the last tree in flower. Snatches of conversation drift above Henrik's head as he slumps against the mermaid's arm, struggling to keep his eyes open.

Bartram plays with Inga's amber necklace, tangling his fingers through the chain. He tugs her forward; she laughs uncomfortably and pulls away. Henrik can make out red marks where the chain digs into her neck.

With one nail, the mermaid reaches up to the tight collar of her borrowed dress and slices it open through the threads of the clasp. With her other hand, she strokes Henrik's hair.

She begins to sing.

Bartram falls silent, his face pale. Inga's mouth drops open.

But the noises of nighttime—the bugs, the windy grass, the harbor—continue on. No sudden magical silence descends. No echo sounds.

The mermaid's voice is pretty in the mid-ranges, but it rasps on the high notes and struggles to find the low notes. Henrik hears better singing at Sunday services, but he likes the tune: jumpy and curious, like a country dance. Instead of words there are empty vowels, like a baby's cooing.

Her mouth hangs wide open like a fish on a line. She beams like a sailor singing for the sake of singing.

Bartram stands up, clinging to the tree behind him. "Let's go home, Henrik," he says, voice wavering. His expression is curled with disgust and his body is angled away from the group, ready to move.

"What? Why? I'm not tired."

"Come *on*," Bartram says, mouth a thin line. He pulls Inga to her feet so roughly she nearly falls over again. "You, too. Faster."

The air feels suddenly hotter. The mermaid sits with her legs folded awkwardly beneath her, gazing up at Inga's necklace with her wide black eyes.

When they leave the mermaid stares after them, mouth vast and unclosing, singing her rasping song.

***

"I'll walk you both home," Inga says quietly. She takes Henrik's hand. The church rises up behind them, a dark spot against the stars. The mermaid's song faded away some time ago, too unformed and juvenile to leave a melody stuck in Henrik's head.

"Why'd we leave her?" Henrik asks. "Does she know her way back?"

"She'll be fine," Bartram says, voice sharp and brittle as a broken shell. He walks before the other two, thin shoulders stiff.

"But—"

"*Henrik*," he says, miserable. "Stop talking."

"But we know she's not a siren! She's nice to me! She's happy and nice!"

Bartram doesn't answer.

Slowly, his walk manifests a twitch. He moves forward at a stumble, his torso pulling forward and his breathing growing heavy. Then he stops walking. He pats down his jacket, increasingly frantic.

"The—the bodkin. Mama's bodkin. I must have dropped it."

"She won't be that mad."

"Go home, Henrik," he says, voice flat. "I'll be back soon." Then he brushes past the two of them, back towards the grove.

"Hey!" Inga says, grabbing for his wrist. "Where are you going?"

He shoves her—"Damn it all, go *home!*"—and breaks into a trot. His fists clench up when he runs. His stride is unathletic, unpracticed.

Inga and Henrik wait in silence together for what feels like a very long time. The church chimes the hour. Their shadows shorten, gibbous moon shining overhead.

Inga says, "Your brother used to be so nice to talk to." Then she begins to run after him.

The two of them pad as ghosts down the darkened road, watching the outskirts of town again give way to the edges of the cherry grove.

Soon, a scream rips through the night air, coming from the mermaid-dock. The sound rises, stutters, and breaks, cutting off at the crescendo.

"That's him!" Henrik gasps.

They scramble and slide down the path to the water. Henrik trips and smashes his head into an exposed tree root. When he stands, his ears are ringing and his head pulses with pain.

Inga has left him behind. Henrik stumbles forward, feeling his way along a wide outcropping of rock.

"She's a monster!"

Henrik rounds the corner. The path widens into the private little inlet. First he sees only loose rocks, fog, water, and foam. Then he raises his eyes to see his brother standing at the base of the mermaid-dock, clutching Inga's shoulders. His eyes are wide, his face close to hers. His stance is off-kilter, favoring one leg.

Henrik notices the blood staining Bartram's arm the same time he feels the warm tickle of it against his own eyelid. His forehead stings.

"She's a monster!" Bartram says, spit flying at Inga's face, slender hands crushing her shoulders. "She called me, she *wanted* me!"

"Bartram," Inga says. The words seem to force their way out of her stomach like meat turned bad: "Did you try to hurt her?"

"What?" He looks startled, a stain of desperation in his eyes.

Her voice turns cold and unfamiliar when she says, "Your belt is unbuckled."

Silence furls out between them with the fog.

"It wasn't my fault," he says, releasing her. He snaps his attention to Henrik. "*You* understand, right? You heard her singing."

Henrik takes a step backwards.

He wants to see his brother's eyes burn, or to see them turn grey as the sea in a storm. He wants to hear the voice of a demon sliding through the tremors of Bartram's words, insidious. He wants to see his fingers bend backwards in impossible directions, see him shrink back from holy water. Then he wants to see him collapse, exhausted but emptied of all evil by exorcism; safe and pure and free.

Instead he sees his brother, as he has always known him: unenchanted, unpossessed, and afraid.

"It wasn't my fault! You heard her sing. She calls men, *tempts* them, pulls them in and destroys them—why else would she sing, if she didn't want me to come? Why else would she be so beautiful?" He reaches out with both hands open, level with Henrik's shoulders; tries to call him into a manly embrace. "Henrik, you understand."

Henrik can't look away. He opens his mouth and closes it again, like a fish stranded on a deck.

Anger burns up in his belly.

"It wasn't *for* you!" he shouts, wavering on his feet. "It wasn't for you!"

His brother casts him such a betrayed look that Henrik nearly takes it back.

"Bartram," Inga says, escaped hair tossing like chain lightning. "You bastard, she just likes to sing."

"She *wanted* me!" Bartram screams, all wounded rage on a choppy sea.

"No!" Henrik screams louder.

All at once the water pulls away from the dock, running backwards over sand and glass and seaweed, pulling loose stones in its wake. Retreating.

Henrik feels his legs give out beneath him.

The sea returns in a black wave.

The dock and the inlet beach are swamped with it. Bartram is knocked off his feet; Inga stumbles back against the rockface. Henrik tumbles beneath the water; feels his back hit the sand.

Thunder sounds. The water drains away again.

The mermaid stands on the balls of her feet at the far edge of the dock. Her toes are curled against the wood; her heels jut out over the water.

She stands in perfect stillness. In her wide mouth there is fire.

The flame sits on her tongue like an egg, just behind her sharp teeth. Smoke drifts up from her lips. When she closes her mouth, the smoke escapes from her nostrils, wreathing her hair.

From her chest—her arms, her legs her forehead—burst auger shells, piercing and splitting her skin before their eyes, pushing to the surface. The skin resists, then tears: where there are no spiking shells, there are smooth stones clustered together in bulging patterns, like rocks slammed together and cemented down by the force of the sea.

She opens her mouth again. The fire pulses between her teeth. A burst of sparks showers to the dock.

Inga screams.

Bartram is already running back up the path, away from the

sea. The mermaid leaps like a whale, arcing impossibly over the entire inlet, over Henrik's head. Sparks and water droplets fall together and sizzle against Henrik's wet skin.

The mermaid pins Bartram to the ground. Bites down on his neck.

Bartram struggles, flails, sobs, crawls on his hands and knees. The two of them drag themselves up the path like a many-legged beast. Henrik still hears the screaming.

He retches into the shallow water still pooled around his knees.

A few rocks shift under his weight. A centipede crawls to the surface, shining wetly in the moonlight. It crawls over Henrik's hand and disappears back into the damp crevice it came from.

Soon the mermaid returns to them, blood running down her chin. The smell of burning flesh hovers in Henrik's senses.

Inga's breathing is sharp and anguished. Her hands scrabble against the rock face behind her. Henrik thinks she's building the courage to run.

The mermaid steps towards her, serene across the rocks, faster than the girl could escape. Her shadow falls over Inga, impossibly long.

When they meet, the mermaid towers over her as she never has before. Inga is trembling.

The mermaid reaches forward, hooking a finger around a length of Inga's hair.

Inga closes her eyes and swallows. Her hands go slack in resignation.

But Henrik sees the mermaid's expression soften in increments:

her forehead wrinkles above her wide eyes, then her jaw unclenches. Smoke stops rising and dissipates.

She looks at Inga's hair as though with pity, noting its well-tended shine.

She drops it, strand by strand, fingers uncurling. Then she reaches up to her own chest and, wincing, breaks off a shell from her body. She places it in Inga's unresisting hand, closing her uncalloused fingers around it.

The shell is the size of a knife.

Three yards away, Henrik curls into himself, retching. He blinks frantically, trying to hold as much of himself inside as he still can.

The sound catches the mermaid's attention. She turns and reaches out to him, then pulls her fingers back as though stung by some possible future. Unease flickers across her eyes.

Henrik forces himself to meet her gaze. He wipes his mouth. He reaches out an open palm.

Then he tastes blood on his lip, and the earth drags him down by the buzzing of his own skull.

The last thing he sees: Inga staring down at the shell in her hand.

He falls asleep, there on the rocks and sand. He dreams of a fish sliding out of its scales, naked and glistening. Tearing itself off of a hook, ripping its wide mouth apart and sliding back into the free sea.

***

Inga lost her amber necklace by the dock that night. She and

Henrik go down to search for it sometimes, though by now they both know it's gone: swept out to the ocean or stolen by a seabird.

The cherry trees lose their leaves as winter creeps in.

"It's alright, you know," she says quietly one day, toeing a bit of ice forming between the loose rocks on the shore. She breaks it down with her boot, rubbing it into water. From there the droplets run back into the sea where they can stay warm.

"What's alright?" Henrik asks.

"If we can't find it." She pats her chest through her thick woolen coat. "I have another one now."

"Didn't your mama give you the lost one, though?"

Inga frowns. She lets her hair down at the dock nowadays, so she has to reach up to rake it out of her eyes when the wind blows. "It's hard to explain," she says. "But my mama gave me...a lot of things. Losing this is alright. Oh—oh, Henrik, it's okay—"

Henrik swallows around the lump in his throat. This happens all the time now—when he thinks too hard about things, or when he isn't thinking of anything at all.

Crying's not so bad, even though he knows Pa wouldn't like it. Sometimes it feels like the entire sea is rising upside of him, saltwater escaping down his cheeks, rivulets staining his lips and soaking there like groundwater.

The bed feels so big now. Years later, the bed will still feel big.

"It's okay," Henrik tells Inga in a watery voice.

She kneels to hug him around the waist.

***

The mermaid doesn't come back to the inlet off the Øresund, even as the years ebb by.

Henrik eats his fish and grows tall—taller and broader than Bartram had. He apprentices himself to a scrimshander, making intricate engravings out of bone and ivory.

"Your hands are too big for that," Mama frets. "You have such big, manly hands. Wouldn't you rather go out to sea with your father?"

"The *Birkholm* sails tomorrow," Pa says, drinking deep from his cup. "Come to the harbor with me and we'll get it all sorted."

Henrik hasn't seen Pa much since Bartram died. He spends more time in town than ever and talks less besides. Sometimes he seems to lose his sight, staring forward into the middle of the room like a blind man. When Mama points this out, he snaps. She cries.

Pa doesn't talk about a lot of things Henrik wishes they could share.

"I'm not coming to the harbor," Henrik says gently. "But I wish you good fortune."

Pa shakes his head and takes a swig. "Then you'll cling to the dirt like Bartram did." His voice breaks on his son's name. "What's happening to this world? No men left in it."

"I wish you good fortune," Henrik says—again, many times, alone.

***

No matter how big, his fingers remain gentle, shaping his

handiwork out of somber, lovely things that were once living. Things taken from the darkened sea.

The practice feels cruel if he thinks too hard about where it all came from. But the sweet, hollow sadness makes him wistful: like mist between blossoms on the edge of the harbor.

Sometimes he asks girls to dance—but only sometimes. Other times he asks them to share their favorite poems with him, or asks them to talk about their dreams. Sometimes he asks of them nothing at all.

He lovingly shapes the bones and feels the sea running backwards inside of him like a wave in the distance.

Pulling back the waters; biding time.

Into the Flames

Jasmine Smith

Jasmine Smith lives in Raleigh, North Carolina where she studies English at NC State University. She can often be found daydreaming new worlds and characters. "Into the Flames" is her first published work.

The palace corridors were littered with the bodies of Laila's friends: the brave men and women who'd decided to give up their lives to protect the Queen. Many of their families had protected the crown for generations. For some, this had just been a good job with a fair employer and reasonable compensation. No matter the reasons, they had all laid down their lives—for nothing.

The Queen was dead. A new one stood in her place.

Laila wished she was dead too.

With every step, Laila came closer to the only room in the palace that remained relatively unscathed from the violence of the night: the throne room. The gilded floor-to-ceiling doors were flung open. Rebels stood at the entryway. Rebel wasn't even the proper term for them. They were more like mercenaries who'd slunk in from the most desolate areas of the continent to pledge their souls for a chunk of change. They wore black and red wood-crafted masks and had axes slung over their shoulders. Blood dripped from the blades, forming a pool at their feet. Laila didn't think she would ever get the metallic scent from her nose.

Within, the tips of palm trees brushed the glass ceiling revealing the glimmering stars of the night sky. Torches lined the edges of the circular room, casting flickering shadows on those who had survived the massacre. The throne itself was separated by a moat of flowing water. It was a golden hollow egg set on a pedestal encrusted with emeralds. Atop the throne sat the murderous queen herself: Aziza.

Laila quickly surveyed the rag-tag group of survivors. She recognized the palace seamstress kneeling beside the head chef and pressing a bloodied rag to his side. A group of five junior guards huddled together. They were only fifteen years old. Their instructors more than likely lay dead in the halls. Not a single member of the Council of Twelve was present. They were locked away in their homes, sleeping safe and sound.

Aziza snapped her fingers and more rebels appeared from the shadows. "My sister—traitor to el-Faiyum—is dead." She held up a crumpled page and dropped it into the rushing water at her feet. "My contacts uncovered a plot to collude with the Khenesian Empire to sell our independence. I could not let this stand." She tapped her fingers against her chin, bathing in the fear that lurked within their silence.

"As the late queen's younger sister and the only remaining child of King Ejikeme, I crown myself your new regent." She balled her fingers into a tight fist and let her gaze sweep across the assembled crowd. "Anyone who rejects my claim will die. But, if you stand with me, we can build el-Faiyum a new, independent future."

Laila waited until Aziza's eyes met hers and slowly knelt down on her knees. She covered her pounding heart with her fist and bowed her head to place her lips onto the skin of her knuckles. Laila had no more tears left within her. Fury burned through her veins. Jamila's reign was over, but Laila's had just begun.

***

Dearest Father,

The Queen is dead…

Before she'd left Khenset, they had agreed Laila would only contact her father in the most dire of emergencies. A government coup seemed like the sort of emergency to warrant a letter. She would need to act quickly to have her plan enacted before Aziza could consolidate her power.

She sealed the letter and tucked it at the bottom of her bag beneath a couple scrolls she needed to return to the temple.

When she reached the streets outside the palace, the air quivered with tension. Soldiers patrolled with clubs and swords. The merchants who normally shouted at anyone who walked along the thoroughfare, stood silently by their carts, only occasionally softly calling to those who passed too close. Laila adjusted her headscarf so that it covered the lower half of her face.

She moved to squeeze into a gap in the crowd when a hand grasped her shoulder. She looked up into a face that was vaguely familiar: dark brown skin and crooked nose. He looked like a man she'd done basic training with. Palace guards didn't normally train with soldiers, but Laila wasn't any normal guard. What was his name? Adnan? Amed?

She lowered the scarf the barest amount. "Yes?"

"Going anywhere in particular?" he asked.

Laila pulled one of the scrolls from her bag. "I need to return these to Sekhet's temple." His eyebrow twitched. "I'm a student of the healing arts." Only half a lie. She *was* a student of the healing arts, but not in this country.

Adnan or Amed stared into her eyes for a long few seconds before releasing her and continuing his patrol.

Laila wound through the city streets. The crowds were scarcer than usual, but still thick enough to conceal her. She caught snatches of conversations swirling around her.

"Queen Aziza has saved us from a life of tyranny."

"Khenset won't be happy."

"She's brought war to our doorstep."

"May our Queen find peace in the afterlife."

But one word remained absent. Murder. They were careful to keep it from their lips with Aziza's spies littering the streets.

Laila ducked into an alleyway and felt along the wall for the loose stone. Once it was dislodged, she slipped the letter into the empty space and checked to make sure no one had seen. Her father's contact checked for messages every evening. She had been silent for so long, she imagined that the messenger would barely know what to do with himself.

***

Two nights later, Laila laid in bed curled up beneath her blanket hiding from the ice-cold draft that swirled around the room. Sleep evaded her. She let her mind drift to a place where Jamila still lived and breathed...

It was coincidence that Laila was in the city. She had just returned from military training in the southern territories when her younger sister appeared at her hip.

"Oh, I've missed you." She crouched down to hug her sister.

Amani was missing one of her front teeth and her sun-kissed light brown hair was done up in loose, fat braids that bounced around her face. "Where is father?"

Amani peered around exaggeratedly. "There's a queen here, but no one's 'sposed to know."

Laila shook her head. Her sister could not keep a secret to save her life. The Empire was vast, spanning most of the continent. Queens were rare; it was even rarer that one would be in Khenset.

"Alright, go play," Laila said. "I'll come find you soon." She watched Amani run into the gardens. The sound of laughter bubbled up as she joined the other children of the nobility. She crept around the perimeter until she reached a seldom used entryway. It was midday, so most everyone was having lunch, or escaping the heat with an afternoon nap. Laila made her way to the center of the palace without being spotted by anyone who could tell her stepmother or brothers that she had returned.

Laila heard her before she saw her. Her voice halted her in her tracks. It was deeper than Laila's. It spoke to her soul like the opening notes of a symphony. When Laila peered around the corner, she was blown away by her beauty. The foreign queen had tightly coiled hair that bounced with every nod of her head. She wore a silver headdress shaped like a swan that nestled on the crown of her head. The swan's beak dipped onto her forehead. Laila stood in the shadows and listened to the tail end of the conversation.

"The goddess has spoken to me and led me here to this point," she said.

Emperor Hassan sat across from Queen Jamila. He nodded and smiled. "Baast only speaks to those who truly believe. We can work together to make this a beautiful world, Your Majesty."

"I think so as well, Emperor."

The next day Jamila traveled back to el-Faiyum—with Laila at her side.

***

The acrid smoke from the pyre brought tears to Laila's eyes. She could almost taste the ashes of her dead queen on the wind.

As a devotee of Baast, it was only appropriate for Queen Jamila's funeral to be held at the temple. Out of the eight gods, Baast was the least worshipped in el-Faiyum. The late king had seen his daughter's devotion as a flight of passing fancy.

The golden statue of the goddess loomed over the crowd, emerging from a fountain at the base of the temple steps. Her eyes were narrow and cat-like. Her face was frozen in a snarl. Baast carried an axe in one hand and a crown in the other, held in a lazy embrace. Laila imagined that if the goddess were to come to life, she would drop it in disgust. What is a crown to a goddess?

The gathering was small, consisting of only the closest members of Jamila's family and friends. Scattered among them were members of the Council of Twelve. Laila could not tell whether they had attended the funeral out of respect for the late Queen or fear of the new one.

Embers flew into the night sky as the pyre collapsed into itself. Laila could no longer make out the maroon shroud that had covered Jamila's body. When the last of the flames died, Baast's servants would collect the ashes and entomb them within the temple, so the queen could rest within the goddess' embrace for eternity.

A murmur ran through the crowd as the Queen's Guard cleared

a path. Queen Aziza took slow, steady steps, leaning on the arm of her handmaiden. A maroon veil covered her face and her waist-length silky black hair was tied up in a scarf. The sleeve of her dress revealed her bare arm, newly tattooed by the priests in the days since Jamila's death. Swirls of gold ink encircled her arms leading up to her shoulders. Laila knew that the skin of her back was inscribed with her vows written in the ancient tongue. If she listened hard enough, she could almost hear Jamila reciting the words herself.

She could feel Aziza's eyes on her through the opaque veil. She stopped just feet from Laila and released her grip on her maiden. Laila fell to her knees before Aziza and bowed her head. Her thick braids shielded her face from view. She clutched her right fist to her chest. "My Queen."

Aziza bent down and took Laila's hand, helping her to her feet. "My sister was incredibly fond of you. I know that you grieve just as much as I do."

Laila's lips tightened. "These are difficult times for us all."

"Speak a few words," Aziza said. "Your memories will bring joy to the hearts of these bereaved souls. Just take care not to excite the crowd too much."

Laila hesitated. Aziza meant to catch her in a trap. To say no would be insolent, to say yes would be dangerous. Even more dangerous would be Aziza's retribution if Laila gave an incendiary speech. "I will tread carefully, my Queen."

Aziza ran her nails along the skin of Laila's cheek. "I will call for you tonight." She leaned close to Laila's ear. Shudders ran along her spine as the veil touched her skin. She could feel the members of the crowd holding their breath, struggling to hear the words Aziza whispered in her ear. "I believe you will find my bedroom most alluring."

Laila turned without a word and followed the path Aziza had left in her wake. She paused before the flames. The air burned all the way down her throat. She could imagine her lungs filling with black smoke, her body combusting from within. She would melt and run down the mountain like soup, drizzling into the streets and sticking to the soles of the workers' boots, being ground down into the soil, and burying herself deep within the earth.

She ascended to the third stair and looked down at the meager crowd below. This was not a funeral fit for a queen. Aziza and her guard had disappeared down the hill. A few of the stragglers shifted from foot to foot. Laila looked to the statue of the goddess. *Give me strength.*

"I did not come here to praise Jamila." Stillness fell over the onlookers. "Queen Aziza has told us of her sister's crimes and they are grievous. She was my friend, but she was not perfect. Which one of us is? Aziza tells us that Jamila's reign would have marked the end of el-Faiyum. Yes, I know. I am a foreigner. Who am I to speak?"

There were nervous laughs from the crowd.

"But, I have lived in this country for three years now, and it has become my home. Jamila's treaty with Emperor Hassan would have threatened el-Faiyum's sovereignty." The ground felt unsteady beneath her feet. Laila closed her eyes to steady herself. "Literacy rates have increased not only in Pri'am, but in the rural areas outside the capital. During the reign of her father, only 40% of the adult population could read. Thanks to Jamila's education reform policies, 90% of our children will grow up to be literate citizens. The construction of the irrigation channels Jamila designed will be complete in a year's time, bringing much needed water to stricken communities.

"She reigned three years and did more in that time than her father before her. And yet, Queen Aziza says that she deserved to die, and we must never question our monarch's intentions."

Laila turned and began to walk up the steps of the temple. She could feel their dagger-like eyes on her back. They would take her speech how they liked. They would run to the Queen or remain silent. She banished those thoughts from her mind. She needed to pray.

***

The palace walls glimmered in shades of red and gold as Laila soundlessly passed through the halls. She had abandoned her funeral garb and was dressed in thick plated armor. Her sword, forged from steel in the palace armory, sat in its sheath at her back. A snarling, full-maned lion adorned her chest plate. Her braids were wrapped in a high bun on her head.

She was given a wide berth as she stalked through the halls, winding her way up through the palace to the Queen's private wing. The guards gave her a solemn nod as she swept past them and into the bedroom that once belonged to Jamila.

The walls were bare. They were once covered in art from the Khenesian Empire that Laila had lovingly curated herself. Colorful masks, abstract paintings, portraits of tribal lands and roaring seas. They were all gone.

Even the furniture was different. Jamila's polished wood cabinets had been replaced with a gaudy white dressing table. Only the bed remained the same. A snarling lioness crafted from stone stared back at Laila from the foot. Sheer curtains were pulled back to reveal Aziza, bare-breasted. Her hair fanned out around her. Her honey-colored skin glittered in the candlelight.

"The Khenesian trash made the perfect tinder." She cocked her head, gazing at Laila, waiting to see her reaction. Laila gave none. She remained standing in the doorway. Aziza stretched out on the bed and arched her back. "How does my body compare to my sister's?"

"I wouldn't know."

Aziza sat up, brandishing a dagger. She sneered at Laila. "Do not lie to me. I will not have a liar in my court." She brushed the tip of the dagger along her finger. "Lie to me again and I'll christen this knife with your blood."

Murder is fine, but dishonesty is where she draws the line, Laila thought. She only nodded and stood perfectly still, taking care not to move a muscle.

"Will you not speak?"

"You called for me, my Queen."

Aziza tossed the knife back on a pillow and stood. She began to pace the strikingly bare room. Her bare feet sunk into the plush carpet. "My sister was stupid to reach out to the Falcon." A shiver ran down Laila's spine. "Those barbarians. They'll take over the entire continent if they're not stopped." She paused before Laila and reached out a hand to cup her cheek. "I have a job for you, love."

Laila inched away from Aziza's hand. "What would you have me do?"

Aziza leaned in and nuzzled her nose against Laila's neck. Every muscle in Laila's body was wound tight. "I want to shore up our defenses," she whispered. "I will show Emperor Hassan that el-Faiyum is not to be trifled with. What better way than to have one of his own leading my army?"

"I'm only a palace guard, my Queen."

Aziza gripped Laila's chin, digging her nails into her skin. "I want you on the front lines, Laila. My sister wasted you." Aziza released her, pushing her away. "Your father is a politician in Khenset, is he not? Can you gleam any intel from him?"

Laila's back was to the door. She rested her palms against the wood, steadying herself. "That can be arranged," she said.

"Good." Aziza sat down at her dressing table and lazily waved a hand. "You may go now."

***

In the morning, Laila found a letter on her dressing table. She opened the curtains and held the envelope up to the light. The black wax of the seal was intact. She brushed a finger over the imprint of the falcon in flight. She ripped open the flap, extracted the paper, and studied the message. When she had committed the contents to memory, she tossed it into the hearth and watched the edges blacken and crumble.

She quickly dressed in an unassuming, plain brown dress and covered her hair in a scarf long enough to partially conceal her face. She left her weapons behind in the trunk at the foot of her bed. The hall was empty when Laila left her room. She slipped down a side staircase and emerged in the back gardens.

The gardens were surrounded by a high stone wall. On the other side lay the city beyond. The paths were lined with flowering bushes and spindly trees with leafy branches to block the piercing sun. At the center was a pond filled with vibrant sunset-colored koi and floating lily pads. Sometimes Laila and Jamila would sit on the benches in near-perfect stillness to watch the frogs jump from lily to lily.

Today, Laila was on a mission. She kept to the edge of the wall, keeping her gaze roving along the path for the palace guards. She had her head turned away when she bumped into a chest covered in bronze. Her excuse sat heavily on the tip of her tongue as she took in the woman standing before her. She was ebony-skinned with closely cropped hair and ears lined with jewels. A silver ring hung from her right nostril. Two spears made an X across her back. She towered a foot over Laila, staring down with an intense glare.

"This is the greeting I receive?"

Laila kneeled down before Baast and kissed her boots. The words had been knocked from her throat. She couldn't think of anything to say. She scrambled back to her feet to find that the goddess' outfit had changed. She now wore a plain dress identical to Laila's. The spears were gone, though Laila knew she never traveled without a weapon. Baast took her hand and led her over to a grassy area near the wall. They sat with their backs against the cool stone in a bubble of silence.

"Jamila is dead."

Baast's gaze bore into her. Laila shrunk back. "As if I don't know," she said. "What is next? Will you bed the woman who killed her?"

Laila jumped to her feet. "If I do, you can strike me down

yourself! You may not believe me, Mother, but I loved her." Her shoulders slumped. "I really did."

Baast opened her arms and Laila fell into them. She buried her face in her mother's neck and sobbed. She hadn't allowed herself to cry since the night it happened, but the door had been opened and the memories were flooding back to her.

Jamila laid in Laila's arms. Her hair was freshly washed and smelled of coconut and jasmine. Laila slid her hand up Jamila's nightgown and caressed her breast. Jamila leaned her head back and kissed Laila's chin.

"I wish I could spend the rest of my life in your arms."

"I wish I could hold you for the rest of my life."

They made love as the candles burned down and collapsed beneath the covers to dream. Laila swore she had only just closed her eyes when the door banged open and Kinsin, the head of Jamila's Queen's Guard entered wild-eyed and wielding a sword. Jamila covered herself while Laila burst from bed and grabbed her knife from the bedside table.

"What is it, Kinsin?" Jamila asked.

"There's been an invasion, Ma'am. It appears the princess is planning a coup."

"Protect this room with your life," Laila growled. She slammed the door in his face and began to dress.

Jamila lay still in the bed. Her eyes were focused on a distant point above Laila's head. "You have to leave," she said, so softly it was almost a whisper.

"What are you talking about?" Laila began to move the dresser in front of the door.

Jamila reached out and grasped her lover's wrist. "There is a secret passageway in the closet. Go now before she gets here."

"You're coming with me."

Jamila shook her head. "No, I'm not." She pulled Laila closer and quickly kissed her lips. "Aziza wouldn't attack if she didn't have at least partial backing of the council. If I am to die, I will not allow her to stab me in the back while I run. Get word to your father. Live, for me."

Shouts sounded in the hall. Jamila jumped from bed and shoved Laila into the closet and then she kneeled before the foot of the bed and waited. Laila felt for the trapdoor in the closet's back wall and soundlessly slid it open. Through the crack in the door, she could see when the soldiers busted down the door, sending the dresser toppling down. Their swords gleamed red with the blood of the Queen's Guard. And behind them came Aziza dressed in a floating white dress with the crown atop her head: a golden circlet of leaves embedded with rubies and diamonds.

"You would betray your own flesh and blood for your ambitions, sister?" Jamila's voice was soft, but it stopped everyone in their tracks.

Aziza smiled and took a small blade from one of her soldier's hands. "I would do it over and over again." One hand yanked Jamila's head back by her hair and the other slid the blade across her throat. Blood sprayed across Aziza's dress, staining the white fabric red.

Laila collapsed into the passageway and stumbled in the dark for what seemed like an eternity. Her legs fought against her. Every *fiber of her being told her to go back into that room, to lie in Jamila's blood and let Aziza's soldiers kill her too. But that wasn't what her love would want. No, she would have her revenge.*

Baast shook Laila's shoulders, bringing her out of her memories. "That's enough," she said. "You can cry when this is over." Baast ran the back of her hand down Laila's cheeks, wiping the tears away. "What do you need me to do?"

Laila was suddenly five years old, sitting in her mother's lap as she sang her to sleep. "Come with me."

"Anything for you."

***

On the western edge of the city sat a dilapidated neighborhood with small wooden shacks nestled one beside the other. A few lone pieces of grass stuck up in piles of dirt served for yards. Beyond was thick forest leading down from the mountains of el-Faiyum to the plains of Aswan and the gushing river that marked the border between the Empire and el-Faiyum.

The forests were filled with traps and soldiers. Most visitors entered the country along the Scholar's Road—mostly traders and academics. El-Faiyum held little interest for most—the country was nothing other than the city of Pri'am and farmland scattered across hills and mountains.

Laila looked around the decrepit surroundings and sighed. Jamila had wanted to create a better life for these people, for her country as a whole. The Empire was a massive influence: nine territories united under one ruler and guided by Baast. Working with Khenset was the only way el-Faiyum would survive. She wanted her people to see them as friends, not enemies.

That would never be.

At the end of the road, closest to the forest, Baast and Laila ducked into the shack and allowed their eyes to adjust to the darkened room. A spear pointed from the shadows. "Ashallay?"

"Maharasha amed," Laila said softly. "Don't you recognize your own sister?"

Rahi emerged from the darkness and enveloped Laila in a hug. "I've missed you," he whispered into her ear.

A lantern was lit, and greetings were exchanged. Rahi's team, two men and three women, bowed to Baast and settled into relaxed stances around the small shack. Baast examined their weapons and the various explosives they had brought. Laila and her brother stood in the doorway. The sharp lines of his face were illuminated in the evening light.

Laila laid a hand on his cheek. "How is your mother? And is father in strong health?"

Rahi shook his head. "You worry too much about everyone else but yourself, Laila. They're fine." He looked away and clenched his fists. "I want to kill this evil woman myself. The Queen was a good woman."

"She was the best." Laila blinked away tears, keeping her mother's words in mind. "But, Aziza's life is mine."

"We've memorized the layout you sent us. I think we're ready."

"You think, or you know."

Rahi chuckled. "I know we are and besides, we have the goddess of war on our side."

Laila looked over her shoulder. Her mother's eyes were already trained on her. Her irises glowed in the dim light. Her skin shimmered. She gave a curt nod and began to dissolve until the only sign of her presence was a pile of gold dust. An invisible wind swept through the open door and whipped it into the air. Baast had fought alongside Laila and Rahi's father on the battlefields, had helped him conquer the surrounding lands and build his empire. She struck down those who stood in his way. But, there was only so much she could do for her daughter. Godly blood flowed through Laila's veins. The Khenesian people called her 'The Blessed Child.'

Laila would be on her own.

***

Laila and Rahi waited until the moon was high in the sky before entering the passageway beneath the castle. They had set explosives at key points along the palace walls—areas where the structure was compromised. The palace guard would be distracted securing the palace from outside threats, while Rahi's team took down the Queen's guard from within. Aziza had planned her coup well. The only thing she hadn't accounted for was the passageway in her closet. If she had been smart, she would have assumed her ancestors would have an escape plan. And why would they tell anyone but their direct successor? The only person Jamila had told about the secret passageway was Laila.

Laila and Rahi crouched just inside Aziza's closet until the ground began to shake. Shouts sounded from the hall, growing more distant as the guards ran to investigate the explosion.

Laila would keep this scene etched in her memory forever: the look of horror that crossed Aziza's face as Laila sauntered from the closet. Aziza stumbled away from her dressing table. Her eyes darted to the door.

"What's the matter, my Queen? Did I frighten you?"

Aziza tossed her hair over her shoulder. She pressed the wrinkles out of her emerald-feathered gown. "Of course not. I thought you might return. I'm actually on my way out." The closet door opened wider and Rahi emerged. Aziza narrowed her eyes. "Who is this?"

Rahi leaned against the door and crossed his arms. "Prince Rahi," he said. "I wish I could say it was a pleasure to meet you."

"Prince...Rahi? As in second son of Emperor Hassan?"

Laila circled around closer to Aziza. She jerked a thumb at Rahi. "My older brother."

Her eyes widened slightly. "You didn't tell me you had royal blood, soldier."

"You didn't ask."

Aziza's hand inched for a drawer and Laila moved, slamming Aziza's head into the desk and jerking her arm up behind her back. "Try. Me."

Aziza sneered. "Do you really think you'll make it out of here alive?" A knock sounded at the door. Rahi opened it and slipped out. "I don't care who your father is. You're in my country."

Laila laughed. "If you knew who my mother is, you would tremble," she said.

"And who would she be?"

Laila leaned down to whisper in her ear, "Baast."

Aziza sniffed, "That explains why my sister liked you so much. You were in with her beloved counterfeit goddess."

Laila threw her across the table. Aziza's head slammed into the mirror before she crashed to the ground. She scrambled up and lunged at Laila, throwing her off balance. Aziza's fist slammed into her chin, jerking her head back. Laila threw her body away, but Aziza snatched a dagger from Laila's belt. She reached out and sliced her arm.

Laila hissed as blood bubbled to the surface. Aziza lunged with the knife, but Laila blocked the strike and kneed her in the abdomen and drove her elbow into her spine. Aziza collapsed.

"I refuse to let you speak about my mother or my lover that way." Aziza tried to crawl to the door, but Laila leaned all her body weight onto her spine. The volume of her voice rose with every word until she was screaming. "Your sister loved me, and I loved her."

She pulled Aziza's head back by her hair. "I just want you to know this before I kill you. You will be the last of your line," Laila said, pulling her dagger from its sheath. "el-Faiyum is no more." She drew the blade across Aziza's throat, splitting the skin and spilling her blood across the carpet.

She tossed the knife to the ground beside Aziza's lifeless body and left the room. She didn't look back. She did not want her memories stained by this. The bodies of the Queen's Guard littered the hall. Rahi conferred with one of his men. When he saw Laila, he crossed to her and pulled her into his arms.

"The army should be here within the hour to secure the city." el-Faiyum would be the tenth territory in her father's empire. Jamila's last gift to her people.

Laila soundlessly nodded and continued walking. She didn't know where she was going. She paid no attention to the servants who streamed through the halls screaming and crying. Word would spread throughout the capital that the Khenesian army was invading. Soon they would realize that the Queen was dead. Laila didn't care. They had stood by and watched as their queen was murdered. One more death would not matter.

She left the ruins behind and walked the streets. Blood dripped from her fingers. Smoke filled the air from a fire burning in the hills. She climbed up the long road to the temple. It was completely dark. The only sound came from the fountain at the base of the steps. Her steps became heavier with each stair she climbed. When she reached the top, she collapsed and lay down on the cold stone. Baast's slender fingers brushed over her daughter's hair and she began to sing a lullaby from times long past.

Laila began to cry as she stared at the blood on her hands. At last.

For Whatever We Lose

Jennifer R. Donohue

Jennifer R. Donohue grew up at the Jersey Shore and now lives in central New York with her husband and her Doberman, where she works at her local library and facilitates a writing workshop. Her work has appeared in Daily Science Fiction, Mythic Delirium, Escape Pod, Truancy, and elsewhere. Her novella "Run With the Hunted" is available on most digital platforms. She blogs at Authorized Musings, where she shares fiction and the tribulations of the writing life, and tweets @AuthorizedMusin.

I lied to meet an astronaut.

Or my dad did, which is the same thing. I was supposed to be at least eight years old to attend, and I was only six but the tallest in my class. So I got to meet the astronaut that August day, instead of going to the beach, or playing in somebody's backyard and running barefoot to the ice cream truck when we heard its roving song.

He was the third man on the moon, and at home I still have the framed and autographed NASA black-and-white of him, young and serious in his spacesuit. It used to be one of the pictures on his Wikipedia page, a piece of my memories out there on the internet for everybody to see. It's probably the same promo photo he used for years; I wonder how many other kids kept theirs? Thinking of it like that makes him seem still alive, like as long as all those pictures are out there, he can't possibly be gone.

I remember him writing his name on the glossy page with a black pen. I remember feeling very important; this was a real autograph, not like the one I got from Mickey Mouse and friends at Disney World in February. He gave some kind of talk, I'm sure. There were a lot of kids there, and I wonder if any of us appreciated it. This man walked on the moon.

Probably, we lied so my dad could meet the astronaut. When I was six, my dad was still kind of a kid himself, just twenty five. I thought of this when I was sixteen and we rented a houseboat on a Florida vacation, so we'd be out in the Gulf and away from light pollution when a shuttle launched at Cape Canaveral. We got up at three in the morning and looked to the north-east for a light in the sky that never came, and we went back to bed. After that, I started to think about maybe being an astronaut. My dad never talked about what he wanted to be.

Every kid who went to see the astronaut was given a mylar balloon that looked like an astronaut in a spacesuit. I don't remember the food, if there was cake or even astronaut ice cream, but that balloon made me happy. It was the kind of balloon that kept its air for a really long time, and I played with it and even talked to it while we were still at the event. It bobbed on its red ribbon behind me as we crossed the parking lot, the sky white with clouds and ready to pour the way it only does in August, leaving the asphalt steaming afterwards and everything hotter and greener and newer.

The car was an oven from our time inside and I put my window down as we drove off. The astronaut was sucked out—red ribbon burning through my fingers—pulled up into the white sky, then too far away to see, just like that. My dad looked back when I started to cry and said "Houston, we have a problem here," but I didn't know what that meant, and didn't get the joke, I just knew my astronaut balloon was gone and I'd never have another one. The idea of *gone* terrified and offended me; it's why I never used stickers, hoarding them instead. It's probably why I used to be afraid of the dark, the yawning darkness that replaced the normal world, that anything could come out of without warning.

Gone was gone, though, and traffic had started to move, so my dad drove on, scanning through the radio stations. I continued to cry, but the watching-what-will-happen-next kind, not the surely-this-will-produce-results kind, and then he stopped on a song and turned it up. "Werewolves of London" always made me smile, and sing along.

We stopped at the liquor store, which sounds like a terrible thing, my dad brought me to the liquor store when I was six. But the liquor store had a seven foot tall werewolf cutout that talked when you stood in front of it, and that's why I liked it there. My dad would never in his life buy that kind of beer, but the radio and that werewolf cutout made losing my astronaut balloon not so bad.

And now I'm grown, older than my dad was that day and, impossibly, my dad is gone too. He and the astronaut both died in the same way: motorcycle accidents. And now I have my own "Houston, I have a problem here," a real one, not just a little girl who's lost her balloon. I'm not crying now because I've trained for this. Years of training, pushing stress levels, staying sharp, staying calm. Plus excess moisture in the cabin would play hell on the equipment, tiny globes salty like the Gulf on that vacation, catching fish that croaked in the air, looking at the night sky. The shuttles are gone now too, mothballed in museums or parked in one of those airplane graveyards in Arizona or New Mexico, safe and dry and dreaming of the sky.

It will take thirteen minutes and forty-eight seconds for Houston to hear my voice and learn my problem. The moon I orbit isn't Earth's moon but one of Mars' mismatched pair, Phobos. My problem isn't going to be fixed with duct tape. My problem is unlikely to be fixed. But I knew the risks, and there wasn't a single step along the way here that was without risk. That's probably why I did it. Six months in a tin can by myself and I had a lot to think about. Like the choices that brought me here. Like the choices that could've kept me home. Would I have joined the Navy in the first place, or been tapped for NASA, if my dad hadn't taken me to see that astronaut? Would I have applied for this mission specifically, if he had lived?

I can listen to "Werewolves of London" almost eight times before I'll hear back from Houston, and they'll probably just say "Copy, Suzanne" while staring at all of their screens, trying to figure out how fucked I am. I never even knew what my dad's favorite song was, just that he hated Bruce Springsteen's "Sandy" and I don't.

It was a perfect sunny day when I got the call. He was already gone; there had been an accident, a terrible accident, and they weren't going to be able to save him. I couldn't get there in time. I couldn't do anything in time. We hadn't talked for awhile, actually, and I'd been thinking about calling him. And then I could no longer call him, I could only go through my saved voicemails in the hopes that one from him was there so I could hear him say my name one last time, but I didn't even get that. I wasn't an astronaut yet, when my dad was still alive. I wasn't on my way to Mars, or to Phobos. I'd hardly logged any flight hours.

I have a laminated picture of me and him on my control panel, from the day I met the astronaut. I'm in a party dress, white frilly ankle socks, black patent leather shoes. My hair in swinging ponytails. I had a particular camera face when I was a kid, a certain smile. When I got older, I didn't even want to look at the camera. After my dad died, I had to relearn how to smile. Judging from internet comments after some of my interviews, I didn't really succeed.

I'm the most alone a human being has ever been. Unless you believe those stories about the Russians, that they accidentally put cosmonauts past the moon, and that amateur radio operators listened in until they couldn't hear them anymore. Gone, like my balloon in the infinite sky. Ghosts on the radio waves, just one example on a list of supposed accidents hidden behind the Iron Curtain. I don't think it really happened. But in my long days which might as well have been nights, it seems far more plausible, and I wonder. I imagine how they might have felt. The differences between us aren't so big, and of course my radio channels are open and waiting at any hour of the day.

"Copy, Suzanne."

I don't say, *Oh, thanks for getting back to me, Houston.* I wait.

Pretty much my mission is a there and back again. Was. Liftoff from 39A at Cape Canaveral six months ago, the shortest time of the year to get to Mars. Settle into Phobos orbit. Deploy some cubesats, takes some pictures. Tool around in a little rover that I leave on the planet-facing side of the moon, to see how shielded from the radiation it will really be. See if the water shielding in my little craft was worth believing in, though of course it must have been or they would never have sent me. Everything five-by-five until I was back on board and some space junk pinged off my service module, putting me into a spin I had to correct manually. Then my power took a heart-stopping dip and when it came back, one of my thrusters was a dented tin can. I pulled an emergency EVA to seal the hemorrhaging fuel tank. My solar array was like an umbrella turned inside-out on a windy day.

In the balance of energy and propulsion, fuel and solar and inertia, there's wiggle room. But not that much wiggle room, not enough to get back home in my lifetime. Fuel conservation and automated systems is one reason my mission is a solo one, and not a duo or trio. And there isn't anybody to come get me, that isn't how any of this works. I orbit Phobos, I will continue to orbit Phobos, even after my power is gone entirely and I am gone too.

When Phobos spirals to the Martian surface, which it will, then I'll be along for the ride. I'm not sure they really considered this when they picked Mars for the next step of humanity, rather than our own moon. An impact that large would be catastrophic on Earth; how different will it be on Mars, if we've been able to install life there? Though Earth's moon is drifting away by infinitesimal amounts, I'm not so sure that's better, or even if it will take longer.

When he was a kid, six or eight or ten, my dad wrote a short story about astronauts who were army guys sent to a different planet, and it turned out there were dinosaurs there. That was popular in science fiction for a really long time, still-living dinosaurs hidden right under our noses. In the middle of the Antarctic, which would also be mysteriously tropical. On the moon, or on Venus. In the sublevels of a department store. No dinosaurs on Mars, though, maybe because our dreams of Mars were consumed, always, by the canals. We know now there weren't canals, but the stories take a certain significance, like we knew water was here somehow and we only just had to keep looking, keep looking.

There is always a chance something like this might happen. There are so many steps along the way where situation normal can suddenly become so very bad. There is the litany of those who have gone before in our bid for the stars. It's amazing there haven't been more, as we strap ourselves into tin cans and fling our fragile, flammable selves into the void. As we compete for the privilege, pushing every last limit. As we return, changed, in every way that might mean. Maybe I thought, if I couldn't do it myself, maybe the universe would do it for me.

At the beach once, when I swam out just a little too far, the current was just a little too strong. I wasn't in any real danger, not like now, but in danger enough, pulled towards the jetty's big black rocks. My dad beat the lifeguard getting to me, and as he got close all I could think of to say was "I'm okay, Dad, I'm okay," possessed of bold, confident calm even at that age. "No you aren't," he said. We sat on the hot sand afterwards, in our towels, and he pretended to be bothered about whether his watch worked. He hadn't had the time to take it off. That watch still works though; still ticking, it hangs around my wrist, one of my few non-essential weight allowances. I never got the band adjusted and by some fluke it doesn't quite fly off on its own if I make a gesture. I don't gesture much in my tin can. I listen to the watch tick, like when an animal is born very small and weak and gets wrapped up with a clock to simulate its mother's heartbeat.

After the funeral I brought my dad's CDs home and listened to them one by one. When I got to *Wish You Were Here*, the case was empty.

"Suzanne?" There's a pause, but they have a captive audience and they know it. "You have a couple of options." And I feel a surge of hope, like every time I change the radio station and in that empty static moment I expect "Werewolves of London". Like when I was too close to the rocks and my dad was there. Like maybe I came to the sky to get my balloon back. But I know this isn't how it works. Being here is impossible, my dad being dead is impossible, and now, so is my return, no matter how gently Houston confirms what I've already accepted. I just hope he would've been proud of me.

The Mare of the Meuse

Janna Layton

Janna Layton lives in Oakland, California. Her poetry and fiction have been published in various literary and speculative journals, including The New Yorker, Apex, Mythic Delirium, Polu Texni, and NonBinary Review.

"We're getting close. I can feel it," said René, and Armand, in that moment, hated him more than he hated anyone ever.

He hated René more than he hated his late father. He hated René more than he hated his late stepmothers. He hated René more than he hated the late Louis XVI. More than he hated the late Marie Antoinette. More than he hated the late Jean-Paul Marat. More than he hated the late Charlotte Corday. More than he hated the living Maximilien Robespierre. All were individual mountains in a range, blocking his path to happiness, one after the other.

"You don't even know where we're going," he snapped.

René was walking ahead as if he were leading their two-person expedition, as if he were the one whose mother lived in Bazeilles, a small town near the border of the Austrian Netherlands. Armand knew that René had never been to Bazeilles, or even its larger neighbor, Sedan. Furthermore, René had the cheek to march along as if he were hardly tired at all. True, he was taller and broader than Armand, but René had been the pampered paramour who lived like a nobleman while Armand was the trained soldier who had marched for years. René had even been in prison longer, and yet had seemingly recovered faster.

"Do you need to rest?" René asked, twirling around, his long black hair flipping over his shoulder. He was smirking, the royalist asshole.

"It's not my fault the guards of La Force treated a baron's lover better than a soldier," said Armand. He put a hand against the stitch in his heaving side, still surprised at how prominent his ribs were. "God knows what you did to get extra bread."

"You really think they treated me better? And anyway, you're one to talk."

"Shut up!"

Armand kicked a pebble, but it promptly bounced off a tuft of grass. René rolled his eyes.

"Let's stop over there," René suggested, nodding towards a copse.

Armand wanted to refuse out of pride, but silently relented. The shade of the trees felt like heaven after the mid-afternoon April sun. Both men were relieved to find a small stream running nearby, probably a tributary from the Meuse River. If so, they were definitely getting close.

Armand quickly stripped off his hated, borrowed clothes: a stained white shirt and the rough, brown pantalons of the revolutionary sans-culottes. When they had escaped La Force, they ran to a friend of René's who scrounged up disguises, food, and a little money before rushing them out at night, terrified of being caught harboring fugitives.

To the pile of dirty clothes on the grass, he added his tattered stockings, the only pieces of his own clothing he had kept.

"So you have energy after all," said René suggestively.

"I'm only going to wash these rags. Don't get ideas."

Still, after both men washed their clothes and then themselves, they ended up in each other's arms in the privacy of the copse.

"We shouldn't be doing this," Armand said as his fingers tangled in René's hair.

He had said something to that effect almost every time they'd had sex since their escape—excepting the first time, when overwhelmed with being out of that house of death, dazed with adrenaline and endorphins, they wildly copulated in an alley.

"According to all those pamphlets," replied René, pausing to kiss a trail up Armand's neck, "the queen and the Princesse de Lamballe enjoyed themselves. So why not you, citoyen?"

"And where are the Widow Capet and Madame de Lamballe now?"

***

"I suppose it doesn't matter," said Armand said after, when they were stretched side-by-side on the grass.

"Mm?" asked René, who was almost dozing.

"Our 'sin,'" said Armand. "What does it matter? Even if it is a sin worthy of hell, what's happening now is hell anyways."

"We've escaped hell. Hell is far behind us. Besides, you told me you're an atheist."

"And it's not just France," Armand continued, his voice quickening and tightening. "It's everywhere. The whole world is losing its mind. This must be the most unmoored time in history."

It was clearly Armand's turn to be overwhelmed. A few nights previously, in an abandoned barn outside Reims, it had been René's. On that night, it had struck René all at once that everything was really happening: no one was truly in charge but chaos, war was everywhere, heads were falling from guillotines by the hundreds, and no one was stopping it. René had felt then that there would never be a remedy, that the world would only get worse and worse. Armand had held him until he had finally succumbed to sleep. Then in the morning, René woke up and the frantic despair was gone, replaced by calm determination. The act of fleeing to escape the murderous machine France had turned into became ordinary again: just something that had to be done, something one did.

Now, naked in the grass, René turned on his side and wrapped his arms around Armand's slim body. Armand let himself be settled so that his head restedon René's chest, the other man's coarse chest hair tickling his cheek. He gazed into the branches of a neighboring tree, where a magpie perched. Its black eyes seemed to be evaluating and planning, and Armand felt a stab of unease at being watched, even though a bird could hardly report them.

"This can't be hell," René said while running a hand down Armand's back, only partly distracting him from the bird's stare. "It's a beautiful April day, there's an extremely handsome young man holding you in his arms, and a breeze is gliding over our bodies while our clothes dry in the sun. Tonight, maybe, we'll get to your mother's house, and then it's on to the Austrian Netherlands, and then to Germany, where we'll be safe."

After the arrest of the royal family, the baron René lived with had sent his wife out of the country while he stayed to safeguard ownership of his lands. The Baroness settled in Coblenz with other nobles, waiting for word that she could return. But now the Baron was dead, and the chateau was the property of the state. René had been disowned by his own family long ago, so going to the Baroness in Germany was all that made sense. How to get there was another matter. While wistfully planning in prison, René and Armand hadn't truly thought they would get the chance to need to work out the specifics.

"What will we do in Germany?" asked Armand. He was still looking at the magpie, which tilted its head to one side, and then other, and then flew off.

"Sleep."

"We'll sleep in Germany?"

"We'll sleep now. We'll figure out what to do in Germany when we get there."

* * *

They woke to a slight chill—the sun was low in the sky. Evening was near.

Armand quickly pulled on his white shirt and handed the red shirt to René. As the other man stepped into old striped trousers, Armand thought of one of the outfits René had worn in prison: silk stockings, light blue breeches, a linen shirt. But despite the expensive materials, René had understandably been in some disarray in La Force. Armand had never seen René's long black hair curled and powdered, only hanging loose and wild like it was now. He thought of the outfits the Baron had dressed René in, which René had described in their hours of tedium: waistcoats embroidered with flowers, a lavender satin jacket, a habit of blue velvet. He wondered what he would have thought if he had seen René at his most dolled up and polished. Was that what René would look like when they got to Coblenz? And would a man like that want anything to do with a simple soldier?

"What are you staring at?" asked René.

"I'm just thinking of how much you must hate those clothes. Obviously they're not what you're accustomed to."

René only shrugged.

"They would not be my first choice. The Baron certainly wouldn't have approved. But a shirt's a shirt, right?"

They gathered their bags and continued walking.

"What is the Baroness like?" asked Armand after a while. "You're sure she'll help us?"

"I think so. She's not as friendly as the portrait by Madame Le Brun makes her look, but she's not mean. A bit haughty, but what noble isn't?"

"She wasn't jealous of you?"

René laughed mirthlessly.

"I should hope not. The Baron is—was—not always a kind man. The less she had to do with him, the better. Really, she owes me for bearing the brunt of him."

Armand felt his stomach clench. "Was he cruel to you?"

René remained silent for a few moments, looking at the ground instead of Armand.

"He took me in when I was just seventeen. He was very generous, but...it doesn't matter. He's gone now. The Baroness and I were never especially close, but she certainly likes me more than she liked her husband."

"But what can she do for us? Her husband's fortune is gone. You said she was staying with friends, right? What makes you think they'll want to take us in? Especially me—I'm the enemy!"

"But you were suspected of being a royalist."

"Only because of my idiot father!"

"We'll just tell them you actually are a royalist. How can they not be charitable to a royalist whose royalist father was executed, and who was nearly executed himself? They'll hang on your every word."

Armand scowled at the idea of presenting himself to simpering nobles as the bereft, loyal son of a martyred merchant who had stood resolutely for the monarchy. What would he say? That he had loved being kicked in the dirt by those above him? Armand was a bastard—his mother had been a maid in his father's house. Once Armand was weaned, his mother was sent back to relatives in Bazeilles, but Armand was kept, as his father's wife had been barren. His father's wife hated him. Then that wife died, and Armand's father got a new wife who also hated him. That wife soon bore a son, and Armand, no longer needed to one day take over his father's business, had been sent into the army.

Armand had only rarely seen his father after that. When he visited, his stepmother glared at him, and his far younger brother pranced around in fancy clothes.

Armand had been quietly gleeful at his father's outrage over the king's imprisonment. After all, the monarchy and their rules were why he, a non-noble, had never been allowed to advance as an officer, despite his clear ability and early education. His proudest moment as a soldier was when he helped repel the royal family's would-be rescuers at Valmy. His father disowned him in an angry letter, which made Armand laugh. He had been newly commissioned as a lieutenant—what did he need his father for? Burning the letter had been satisfying at the time, but he later regretted not having it as evidence.

His father and stepmother were arrested for sending money to émigrés. His father had bawled and begged for his adult son as a character witness, thinking the judges would be swayed to see he was the father of a soldier with Jacobin sympathies. Instead, with paranoia running rampant, doubt had somehow been cast on Armand as well. Armand suspected his stepmother was to blame—when she saw he would not defend them, she must have convinced someone he had been an accomplice.

If the great General Lafayette could be defamed as a traitor, what hope did a bastard lieutenant have? Both his father and stepmother had been executed while Armand awaited his own trial. He didn't know what happened to his half-brother.

Armand was caught up in thought when René stopped him with an outstretched arm. He followed the other man's gaze.

Up ahead of them, against a darkening green field and the lavender sky, a horse grazed.

That was striking for several reasons. The first was that the horse itself was eye-catching: it was a piebald, its coat composed of large splotches of black and white, like a map of seas and continents. The second was that the horse was saddled and bridled, even though no rider appeared nearby. The third was that, even though Armand tried to convince himself it was simply a fallen tree branch situated at an angle near the horse's grazing head, the horse had a horn.

"It's a unicorn," whispered René.

"Don't be stupid," said Armand. "There is no such thing. A cruel prankster has glued something to the poor animal."

The horse raised its horned head and looked at them. Then it let out a loud whinny.

"It's seen us," said René, pushing Armand behind him.

Armand had a moment to feel annoyed (true, he was smaller in build, but of the two of them, he was still the soldier) before the creature started trotting towards them. Suddenly, Armand could not be as sure as he had been that this was just a horse with an ornament attached to its forehead. Instead, he could picture the long horn skewering them both. After all, according to legend, only virgins could safely subdue unicorns, and neither he nor René qualified. He grabbed René's arm and started to run.

"This way," he ordered, pulling René in the direction of another cluster of trees in the distance.

They could climb a tree. Would that deter the unicorn from attacking them? How high could unicorns jump? Could unicorns fly? Armand hadn't noticed any wings, but who knew what a real unicorn could do? No, he told himself. What was following them was not a real unicorn. It was a victim of young men's humor. Honestly, a horse made to look like a unicorn sounded like something the idle nobility would demand for a party, assuming there were any still alive. But Armand heard the hoof beats and another frantic whinny and couldn't convince himself to stop running.

When he risked a look over his shoulder, to his horror the unicorn was far closer than he thought possible. The beast had started to gallop, and was gaining quickly. Their human sprinting was no match for its stride. Reaching the trees in time was impossible. He shoved roughly at René's shoulder.

"Keep going," he shouted, and then turned to face the monster alone.

"What are you doing?"

"Just run, idiot," gasped Armand, out of breath. "I'll fight."

"You'll fight a unicorn?"

"I'll delay it. Just get to the trees."

To Armand's absolute fury, rather than running off to safety and leaving Armand to die a hero's death at the horn of the unicorn, René hefted him over his shoulder. Even with his upside-down vantage point and René's ass in the way, Armand could see it was too late, anyway—the unicorn skidded to a stop beside them. Armand braced himself for death.

Instead, the unicorn knelt down on one knee, the tip of its horn resting against the earth.

René backed up in confusion, and Armand successfully launched himself off and staggered to his feet. For a few moments, the two men just stared at the creature, which seemed neither fully unicorn or fully horse.

Rather than being deer-like in stature and white in coat like the unicorns depicted in paintings and tapestries, the piebald unicorn was the size of a large cart horse. Unlike a cart horse, or any horse, its coat gleamed with a faint iridescent sheen, like the nacre of a seashell. The horn looked like a spiral of black and white marble.

René took a step forward.

"Don't," hissed Armand.

"I'm going to touch it."

"Why?"

"To see if the horn is glued on."

René knelt down alongside the creature and stroked its neck.

Nothing happened. Then he carefully touched the horn, grasped it, and tugged a little. Armand flinched, but the unicorn didn't react.

"It's a real horn," said René. "And look, a pillion saddle, so two can ride."

The idea that the unicorn had been prepared with them in mind alarmed Armand, and he suddenly remembered another legendary animal a fellow soldier had told them about around a campfire.

"It's the Cheval Mallet!"

"The what?" asked René, looking up at him.

"The Cheval Mallet. A soldier from Vendée told me about it," said Armand, the details flooding back to him. "It's a black horse who comes to weary travelers at night. It's saddled and bridled, and kneels down like this. The traveler mounts the horse, and it gallops off with him, never to be seen again."

"And you believe that?"

"I didn't until now, but it has to be that. Get away from it," he urged, pulling René to his feet.

"This is a unicorn, though. Was the legend about a unicorn or a horse?"

"Does it matter? For all you know, this creature was sent by the devil himself."

"Again, you're an atheist, and why would the devil send us a piebald unicorn? Maybe it's sent from heaven."

"Why would heaven send us a piebald unicorn? And yes, I am

usually an atheist, but look at it! Maybe our world has fallen so far, with so much depravity and bloodshed, that demons are rising to devour it."

René regarded the unicorn for a moment, and then made the sign of the cross. The unicorn didn't seem to care. Slowly, he circled the animal.

"It's a mare," he remarked.

"We should go," said Armand.

"Should we tell someone about it?"

"We're fugitives. Whom can we tell? Let's get out of here."

The two men continued on their way.

The unicorn followed.

At first, Armand said they should just ignore the creature. Eventually, he hoped, it would get bored and wander elsewhere, looking for other travelers to tempt and carry to their doom. When that didn't work, Armand tried making shooing motions with his arms, and then ordered it sternly to stop. René tried orders in English and Italian, but the unicorn didn't respond to that either.

Soon it was dark, they were nearing the road to Bazeilles, and the unicorn was still right behind them. As a last-ditch effort, René dared to touch the potentially cursed reins and looped them over the low branch of a tree. That worked. The unicorn stood patiently by the tree as René and Armand left.

They walked to the road, looking over their shoulders occasionally to see if the unicorn was following them. It was too dark to ascertain that it was still where they left it, but at least it wasn't at their heels.

"It feels wrong to just leave her there," said René.

"That strange beast is not our problem."

Even though it was dark and Armand had only been able to visit his mother a handful of times in his life, he knew they were getting close to the bridge into Bazeilles. Then it was a short walk to the small stone house on the outskirts where his mother lived with her brother's family. Every time he visited her, when she first saw him approach her face would light up as if she were witnessing a miracle. How would she look at him tonight, when the last she had heard of him was a smuggled letter months ago, telling her he had been arrested? His feet seemed to speed up of their own accord, and he felt something primal calling within his chest. After months of confinement and despair, he was headed to his mother's arms. Any doubt he had about fleeing in this direction with René disappeared—he would be safe soon.

However, as they neared the bridge, he saw something he hadn't expected: a light. He and René stopped for a moment, and then through mutual, silent agreement, crept slowly forward. From the light of the full moon and what turned out to be two lanterns, they could see two figures on the bridge. Were they guards, or just citizens chatting? Armand held a finger to his lips, then gestured for René to follow him. Slowly, carefully, they crept closer to the bridge, staying behind a row of bushes and trees.

Finally, they were close enough to hear the two men talking.

"I always hated that ornery goat anyway. If someone took it, good luck to them."

"I doubt it's been stolen. Who would want it? That old thing probably just ran off for greener pastures. It could have been the 'unicorn' Cassandra du Moulin claims she saw this morning."

"Ha! Who knew the Moulin girl would turn out to be crazy? What a waste. But enough gossip; I should head home. Good luck with the watch. I haven't seen any unicorns or Austrians tonight, and I doubt you will either."

One man left with his lantern, leaving the other standing guard with his own. René and Armand retreated until they were far enough away to whisper safely.

"What can we do now?" fumed Armand.

"We can go farther along the river and swim."

"I can't swim. You can?"

René nodded. "The Baron's chateau had its own lake. I'll help you across."

"Are you crazy? I'll pull you under."

The two contemplated the situation for a few moments.

"You know," said René, "We do happen to have access to a mount."

"That's an even worse idea."

***

The unicorn was where they left it, and made a soft, seemingly happy whicker when they approached.

René patted the animal's shoulder and took up the reins. Once again it lowered itself to the ground, waiting for them to get on, but René pulled it up and started walking. The unicorn walked calmly at his shoulder.

Armand followed on high alert at first, keeping one hand tucked into René's waistband in case the creature tried to drag him to lands unknown, but eventually his mind wandered. It had been a long, strange day after many long, strange months, and Armand was eager to get to the house. Soon he would see his mother. She would embrace him. He and René would be fed a real meal and sleep on a real bed.

A bed. That thought gave him pause. He and René had slept together every night since their escape. They had slept in a hay-loft, bushes, grasses, a chicken coop, a shed. In all of these places they had slept intertwined, but they had never slept on an actual mattress together. As guests, they would be given his youngest cousins' bed, and there they would rest side-by-side, warm under a quilt. Although he reminded himself that their pairing was one of convenience, the thought made his heart beat a bit faster.

Of course, then René said something that annoyed him.

"I think we should name her."

"Oh? And I suppose you have a name already?"

"I was thinking of Orinda."

"What kind of name is that?"

"She was a British poet. A royalist," René said, turning so Armand could see his smirk.

"What an appropriate name for a beast from hell."

They walked away from Bazeilles, far from the bridge, and found a calm, secluded place to cross the Meuse.

"All right," said René. "Let's take off our clothes and shoes and put them in the bags. You'll be alongside Orinda with one arm around her neck and the other holding our bags above the water."

That was their plan, and it had seemed an acceptable way to avoid actually riding the unicorn and risk being carried off to an uncertain fate, but now looking at the dark water, Armand was frightened.

"Come on," René urged, stripping his own clothes off for the second time that day.

Armand reluctantly undressed, and soon they were both naked in the moonlight, their feet bare on the ground.

"If this unicorn is anything like a regular horse," said René as they walked down the bank, "only her head will be above water, so you'll have to hold her neck very high up. This would be easier if you would just sit on her."

Armand shook his head. Even though he had sneered at the Vendeean soldier's story of Cheval Mallet disappearing with its riders, he couldn't get the image out of his mind. Why else would this mount be waiting for them with tack, tempting them? What they were trying was foolish enough.

They started wading into the cold water, René holding the reins on the unicorn's left and Armand just behind him, one hand on the unicorn's withers. The water reached their knees, then their hips. Armand felt a spike of panic. He had never purposefully gone into deep water like this.

René kept glancing over his shoulder every few steps, checking Armand's progress.

"You're doing well. It gets deeper up here. Get your arm around Orinda's neck."

Now that the moment was close, Armand couldn't picture himself successfully keeping his head above water with only one arm holding him up.

"Wait!" he cried.

"What is it?"

Armand knew his face was beet red, and he was glad René couldn't see that. He hated asking for help. "Can you take the bags?"

"I'm holding the reins."

"I can't...I need both arms," Armand stammered, his voice weaker than he wished.

René assessed the situation, then agreed and took the bags, giving Armand the reins to hold.

"Wait here," he said. "I'll come back to help you across."

Armand held the reins as lightly as possible and watched René kick across the river in the moonlight, more or less keeping the bags out of the water. How did he make it look so easy, like swimming was something humans should know how to do naturally? It was too dark to see the opposite riverbank, but soon René swam back and took up the reins again.

"Ready?" he asked.

Armand nodded, but his heart was pounding. They started moving forward once more.

The moment Armand's feet no longer felt the mud and rocks beneath them was one of terror. He turned towards the unicorn, wrapping both arms tightly around her neck, glad he had made René take the bags. Then the riverbed disappeared from beneath the unicorn's hooves as well. Her legs started churning, and suddenly the water was up to his chin. Some splashed in his mouth, making him cough.

"I'm drowning!" he cried.

"You're all right," René insisted over the splashing. "We're half-way there."

Armand couldn't judge if René was telling the truth or not. All he could see was the unicorn's neck, darkness, and splashes of white. Then he and the beast bobbed down and his whole face was submerged.

Cold water poured up into his nose, burning. His eyes opened, but he could see nothing. Automatically, his arms started thrashing, letting go of the unicorn's neck. With nothing anchoring him, the current began to drag him away. He tried to scream, but more water flooded his throat. He reached out his hands but found nothing to grasp. He couldn't hear anything except a low roar. He didn't know which way was up. His lungs were going to burst.

He wanted his mother. She was so close, closer than she had been for so long, and yet he could not call for her. He was going to disappear, a corpse carried far along the Meuse, and his mother would never know.

Something struck his arm. He twisted his wrist to grab it, and found something slender but solid in his palm. Was it a branch, an oar, a shepherd's rod? His other hand reached the lifeline, and he clutched it tighter than he had gripped anything in his life. Before he could even start pulling himself up, he was being lifted.

He gasped as he re-entered the cold night air, coughing up water.

What he was grasping was the unicorn's horn. The strain must have been enormous, but she was holding him up. René appeared and grabbed him by the waist, saying something he couldn't understand, and then his soles started brushing mud and rocks again. It had never felt so vital to have ground under his feet.

René helped Armand up to the safety of the riverbank, where he collapsed, still coughing. His nasal cavities, throat, and lungs all burned, but he was freezing and trembling. Then he was being held tightly in René's strong arms, pressed against René's broad chest, and the man was murmuring softly to him. He could feel the soft nose of the unicorn nuzzling at his shoulder, warming his skin with her hot exhales.

"That was stupid idea," he said when he finally got his voice back.

"But we made it," René said.

Then Orinda shook like a wet dog, splattering water over them again, making René laugh and Armand swear.

"Thank you, Citoyenne Orinda," Armand said, wiping his face.

Soon they were dressed, and René was once again hitching Orinda to a tree.

"It feels even worse to leave her this time," he said, stroking the shimmering neck. "We're just going to let the townspeople find her in the morning?"

"I'm sure she can take care of herself," said Armand. "She must have that horn for a reason."

However, he had to give the creature a pat as well. He still wasn't completely convinced she wasn't the Cheval Mallet, but she had saved his life.

They walked through the darkness, Armand leading the way. He wanted to cry out when they reached the small house where his family lived, but as to not attract undue attention, Armand knocked quietly.

He had to try a few more rounds of knocking, but the door finally opened, and there stood his uncle with a candlestick. The man stared at Armand for a few moments in confusion, then pulled him inside.

"What are you doing here?" he hissed, shutting the door behind René. "Have you been released?"

Directly through the door was the family's cramped main living area and kitchen. The dark house was mostly lit by a fire in the fireplace. Armand's aunt and his cousin sat at a rough table, their faces illuminated by another candle.

"Armand," his aunt said, rising.

She sounded stricken, confused.

"Your hair is wet," said his uncle. "Did you swim across the Meuse?"

"Forgive me. I know this is a surprise," said Armand. "My friend and I are on our way out of the country, and we hoped to stay here for the night. Where is my mother?"

There was a long silence, and he could see the answer on his family's faces, but he didn't want it to be true. He told himself the low light altered their expressions.

"Armand," his aunt repeated hesitantly, "we weren't expecting you."

"Where is she?" he asked. "Is she asleep?"

René must have figured it out too, and lay a hand on Armand's arm. Armand angrily shook it off. His mother must be in the small room she shared with his eldest cousin. He stepped towards the hallway that led to the home's three bedrooms, but his uncle took his arm.

"Armand, I'm sorry," the man said gravely. "We thought you were to be executed soon and did not want to tell you."

"No," he said, pulling his arm away.

"She fell ill a month ago. The doctor said it was an infection from a bad tooth. He pulled it out, but it was too late."

"No."

His family members only looked at him with anxious, uncomfortable faces, so René guided him to a chair near the fireplace and knelt at his feet, holding his hand.

"She was trying to save money to go to Paris," said his cousin Adele, belatedly hurrying over from the table to offer comfort. She was the eldest girl, nineteen, herself an unwed mother of two boys who were presumably sleeping in the children's room. "She wanted to go speak on your behalf. She knew you were innocent."

Armand stared blankly into the fire and imagined his mother—a slight, illiterate woman who worked in a cloth factory—setting aside her few coins to try to save her son from the guillotine.

"And who are you, sir?" his uncle asked René.

"A friend of Armand's."

"Another prisoner?"

Armand heard the suspicion in his uncle's voice. Because of his father, he assumed, his uncle had never been fond of him.

"You can't stay here, you know," his uncle continued gruffly. "If you're found, it's the guillotine for all of us."

"Papa," Adele cried, "he has only just learned about his mother, and they've come all this way. And what about the monster that was seen nearby?"

"There's no monster, Adele," scolded her father. "Cassandra is a liar."

"Your father is right. You want your children to be orphans too?" her mother asked. "Did anyone see you come in?"

"No," René said, rising and standing between Armand and his aunt and uncle. "We were incredibly careful. No one has seen us. Please, if you would just let him stay the night. He's had such a shock, and nearly drowned crossing the river. I'll take care of him. We'll leave tomorrow night, under cover of darkness."

"Listen to the way you talk," said the uncle, regarding René carefully. "Like Armand did back when he was living with that rich father of his. You're no worker. You probably stole those clothes off a laundry pile somewhere. What are you? A marquis?"

"I served in a nobleman's house," said René, "but I am not a nobleman."

"That won't matter to the Committee of Public Safety," said the uncle, "especially if you fled prison. I am sorry about your mother, Armand, but you must leave at once. I won't have my family executed for this."

"At least let him warm up," begged René.

But his uncle had become adamant that they must leave immediately. With the unspoken threat that he would report them
himself, there was nothing Armand and René could do but
acquiesce. René led his nearly catatonic companion to the door.

"Wait," said Adele.

She grabbed a candlestick and hurried off down the little hallway. Soon she reappeared holding a green, wool cloak. Armand
recognized it immediately. Using his small soldier's salary, he
had bought it for his mother for Christmas a few years back.
How happy it had made her. When Adele handed it to him, he
held it wordlessly to his chest.

"It was his mother's," Adele explained.

"Thank you," René said.

Defeated, the two men walked back towards where they had left
Orinda. René kept his arm around Armand's shoulders.

"What do we do now?" Armand finally asked.

"We can still go to Germany," said René.

"Is that really where you want to go?"

René did not answer.

Orinda came into view, and although she was still otherworldly
with her glittering black and pearlescent white coat, Armand
was struck by how familiar she seemed already. The sharp horn
he had imagined skewering him only hours earlier had since
been used to save him.

The mare greeted them with a soft whicker and René patted her neck. Armand stared at her piebald markings, imagining if they really were a map to lands and oceans unknown.

"I wonder if it's true—that if we mount her, she'll take us far away from here and we'll never be seen again," said Armand.

"Do you want to try?" asked René. "Maybe we can go anywhere."

"Why not?"

He secured his mother's cloak around his shoulders while René latched their bags onto the saddle. Sensing her moment had at last come, Orinda knelt down as she had when they first met her.

"Ready?" René asked.

Armand nodded.

René boosted him onto the saddle, and then Armand scooted back onto the pillion so that the better rider could sit up front. As René settled into the saddle, Armand wrapped his arms around his waist and focused on how the heat of the other man's body warmed him where they touched. He focused on the weight of his mother's cloak on his shoulders and remembered how it had felt to be held by her. He looked up at the bright full moon, the numerous stars. *If I'm about to die*, he told himself, *let these be my last thoughts.*

Then the mare began to rise to her feet, and he closed his eyes, resting his forehead against his lover's shoulder.

A Promise of Apples

J.S. Rogers

J.S. has been writing since she could get her hands on a pencil and paper. These days, she writes as a freelancer for her day job and pens fiction by night. Her fiction has appeared in print and around the web.

Deirdre slipped from the family's cottage with the setting of the sun. Mother knew she went, she must have, trying as she was to soothe baby Aileen's hungry fussing. Mother neither said anything, nor looked towards her as she stepped out into the dark night. The moon hid her light behind grey clouds, turning even her face away from them.

The first snow covered the earth, though that meant little. There was no crop this year, nothing to fill their bellies. They had none since they lifted the first of their potatoes the previous year and found it blighted, just as the papers had warned.

They had scraped and scrounged for food for over a year, but there was little and less of it. For them, anyway. Crispin, their landlord's man, overseer while Sir Daven glutted himself in accursed England, seemed fat and happy enough. His round-cheeked daughter did not weep for the ache in her gut. The crops they grew for him; the sweet wheat, the peas, and beans, he packed neatly. Most had been sent away, off to the ports in the south and to tables in England. But some remained, stored and waiting.

Deirdre meant to liberate those stores.

She moved through the night to the storehouse quietly. She knew these fields and these hills; she had never been elsewhere in her seventeen years. She would break into the stores and take all she could carry. They could hang her afterwards, if they wanted. The food would be enough to get Mother, Colleen, Sean, and Aileen south, to a ship and a better life.

To any life at all.

Deirdre circled the copse of oak trees near the cattle pen, her mouth watering at even the thought of meat, and a whisper of music on the wind came to her ears. Soft and sweet, the music came from within the trees. She could not imagine who would be playing on such a cold, lightless night. Nor could she imagine why anyone would dare venture into the oak trees. Mother had always warned against it. Still, the music made her hesitate, even with hunger eating at her stomach.

It had been so long since she heard music. The notes drew her forward, under the boughs of the trees, dark and bare from the onset of winter. Mist hung among the branches. A bird fluttered overhead, stirring wisps of fog. Deirdre ducked under a branch, stepped over a root, peered around a twisted trunk, and found a woman.

Her breath caught. The woman sat, legs folded upon the cold earth, clad in fabric that shimmered in the dark. Her hair fell over her shoulders in dark curls, pooling around her legs on the bracken. Her skin was pale as moonlight, her face round, her nose upturned. She held a silver flute in her slim hands. A spring burbled beside her, one Deirdre had never seen. She never dared come into the woods before.

A branch broke beneath her foot and the woman stopped playing, her eyes snapping open; such eyes they were, huge and dark and shining. "My apologies, miss," Deirdre blurted, sketching a hurried curtsy. "I did not mean to disturb you."

The woman stood, her skirts whispering against one another, taller than Deirdre expected her to be. She eyed Deirdre, who rubbed her palms down her skirt. "I've not heard music in some time," she said. "You have a talent for it."

The woman cocked her head to the side and then smiled at Deirdre. She said, "Come and sit. Eat. I will play for you some more."

And Deirdre saw that a blanket was spread across the ground, piled high with fruits and breads, with butter and fresh milk, with a pie that steamed in the cold air. Spit flooded her mouth and her gut clenched. She knelt by the blanket, her fingers closing around a firm, red apple. She brought the fruit to her mouth, teeth aching for it, and stopped an instant before biting into the crisp flesh.

The woman stood over her, watching. Her dark hair fell over her shoulder. Her bare arms were long and lean. The cold seemed not to touch her. A circle of toadstools surrounded them and the spring. Deirdre lowered the apple—a trial—and swallowed.

"You're one of the fair folk," she said, cold and dread finding a home inside her ribs.

She stared down. "Do your folk still remember us, then?"

"Aye," Deirdre said, thinking of Mother back home, of her brother and sisters. Would they think she had abandoned them if she did not return, if the lady swept her off to the faerie courts? "We remember. Please, my lady, will you let me go?"

"You are hungry," she said, and Deirdre's eyes fell on the array of food. There seemed more of it: a roasted chicken sat by her knees, a bowl of soup sat beside it. There was not a potato to be found. She nodded. "You are *all* hungry."

"We are," Deirdre said, for at least she still spoke, at least the world around them had not changed, though she had been so foolish as to step into a faerie ring. "Lady, I beg you, let me leave."

"You mean to steal food to feed your family," she said, matter of fact. Her voice sounded like music. Deidre winced at the beauty of it. "It will only soothe their bellies for a few days. And you will hang, when they catch you."

Deirdre balled her hands into fists, pressed against her legs. She felt the bones beneath her skin. "Perhaps," she said. "But—"

"I have watched your people since this world was young," the elf-woman said, sitting once more. She reached for the apple Deirdre had held and bit into it. Saliva flooded Deirdre's mouth. Her stomach gurgled. The elf-woman held out the fruit, the contrast of red skin against her white flesh striking. "Eat," she said. "There is plenty of food in my realm."

"You would trap me," Deirdre said. The elf-woman just stared, her beautiful features impassive. Time stretched. Deirdre's stomach rumbled. She would be caught. Everyone knew that if you ate of the food of the fair folk they would have a hold on you forever. But. She licked her lips. "Would I be treated well?"

The elf-woman tilted her head to one side. Her eyes were dark, dark and deep. Old. She said, "You would not starve."

Deirdre shivered.

Hunger ate at her thoughts. Aileen's skeletal arms waved in her mind. The stores waited in the barn. A few days of food would not spare Aileen's life, or give the others the strength to reach a port. She swallowed saliva, terrible fear of the options set before her twisting in her stomach. She said, finally, "You say you have food. Food for how many?"

***

Mother looked up with hollow eyes when Deirdre returned. She held Aileen close, the girl finally fallen into a miserable sleep. "You must come with me," Deirdre said, gripping Colleen's bony shoulder and shaking her awake, moving on to Sean. "Right now."

"Why?" Mother asked, but she rose carefully. Deirdre knew not how she held onto Aileen, thin as she had become. Colleen and Sean rubbed at their eyes, empty-cheeked.

"Because I do not know how long she will wait."

"Who?" Colleen asked, swaying when Deirdre threw her cloak around her shoulders.

"Come quickly now," Deirdre said, guiding Sean out of the door. She took Aileen from Mother, startled by how light the babe felt and the bird-fast beating of her tiny heart. Deirdre would have struggled to hold her, earlier in the day.

"Deirdre." Mother's fingers squeezed around her arm, the tips of her thumb and middle-finger touching. "What do you mean to do?"

"I mean to see us all fed," Deirdre said, swallowing. She could see the fear in Mother's eyes. And the hope.

"How?" she asked, quietly.

Deirdre's tongue tangled around the words. Her jaw ached. But she found a way to speak. "I went into the oak trees," she said.

Mother drew in a sharp breath through her nose, her fingers bit into what remained of Deidre's flesh like claws. "I heard music. And there was a woman there, and—"

"We cannot eat her food," Mother said. "Those who eat the food of the fair folk are theirs. We would be taken away, never able to return—"

"What is there to return to?" Deirdre asked, the first time in her life she had ever dared interrupt Mother. "Besides hunger? Besides a grave near Father?"

Deirdre saw a fire, assumed long-extinguished, flare in Mother's eyes, just for a moment, and thought she would be slapped. But Aileen stirred in her arms, with a whimper instead of a wail, and that fire faded away. "The fair folk cannot be trusted," Mother said.

"I know." Deirdre shrugged. "But is not the possibility of deceit better than the certainty of death?" She felt Colleen and Sean watching them, wide-eyed and sunken-cheeked. She breathed too hard. She wondered what she would do if Mother refused.

But Mother closed her eyes and nodded. "Very well," she said. "We must tell the others."

***

They hurried from cottage to cottage, the back of Deirdre's neck itching with each second that passed. They were met with confusion and disbelief, but hunger beat them to every door. The memory of the dead won their arguments for them. The crowd around them—some little more than walking skeletons—grew and grew, until there were no more failing cottages to visit.

No one turned down their offer.

The trip through the dark went slowly. Colleen and Sean were clumsy and tired, and so were so many of the others. They made noise as they went, until Deirdre's nerves felt fit to burst from her skin. She hushed and hustled them along, past the accursed fields and the cattle paddock, into the oak trees. Music filled the air. Mother shuddered beside her.

Deirdre led the way, around piles of bracken and low branches. Her heart lodged in her throat. She stepped around the gnarled tree, adjusting her hold on Aileen. For a moment she dared not look, but then she opened her eyes.

The faerie woman stood within her toadstool circle. A basket waited beside her, piled high with fruits. She held an apple in one hand. It had two bites taken out of it.

She gazed forward, her dark eyes taking in the sorry lot of them. Her mouth tightened and her eyes narrowed. And then she drew in a breath and her expression softened. "Come, folk of Éire. There is enough for all of you."

Colleen looked up at Deirdre, pressed against her bony side. Colleen's face was pale. Deirdre nodded, her throat too tight for speech, and Colleen darted forward, stepping neatly over the toadstool ring. The fairy woman reached into the basket and offered her an apple. The joyful sound Colleen made when she took a bite brought stinging tears to Deirdre's eyes.

The others rushed forward, then, and there were apples for everyone, and the food brought color back to their cheeks, closed the splits in their lips, and eased some of the emptiness around their eyes.

Deirdre watched them, still tasting the sweet juice of the bite of apple she had taken on her tongue.

"Come," the fairy woman said, when the last of them finished, the whole of every apple consumed, stem and seeds and core and all. "More awaits you."

"Wait," Mother said, staring down at Aileen, awake and not crying for the first time in too long. Tears shone in Mother's eyes, but did not spill down her cheeks. "Why have you done this? Surely you can tell us now. We have eaten your food."

The elf woman looked over them once more. "You think my people to be cruel," she said. "And you are right to think so. But mortals are cruel, too. And we are not monsters. We miss the sound of the laughter of your folk and the way you used to dance. Pain and death are fine things. Necessary things—" she shrugged, "—but only when balanced by life and joy. Come. Eat. Sing and dance once more." And she lifted Aileen then, without any effort, and turned, and when she stepped forward, a path lined by trees with golden leaves stretched out before her.

Warm air blew out against Deirdre's face. She smelled flowers and baking bread. Birds in dozens of colors flittered between the trees. Delightful music hung in the air. There would be trials, she knew. She had heard all the stories. But there would be food, too. And music. And joy. Life, instead of empty death.

Deirdre stepped forward to follow the faerie woman, joined by all her folk.

***

The morning dawned grey and quiet.

No one limped from the cold cottages to scrounge for scraps of food or to see to the cattle, who needed fattening still for export to the tables of Britain. The quietness and emptiness of the day drew out Crispin, who finished a breakfast of quail's eggs, sausage, and rich, dark bread coated in butter before sighing and going to see what new problem awaited him.

He found no workers in the fields. The cattle milled about, waiting to be let out to the grasses that they were yet denied. No smoke rose from the chimney in the nearest cottage. The door stood open. Crispin looked inside, a chill running down his spine.

No one lurked within. No one waited in any of the cottages.

He had went to bed the overseer of forty tenant farmers.

He found none of them in the light of morning. He found no sign of where they had went.

He turned in a circle in front of the last cottage, as though perhaps he would discover them lurking just over his shoulder. He only smelled apples and heard a whisper of music on the air, there and gone again.

At Love's Heart

Amanda J. McGee

Amanda J. McGee is a mapmaker
by day and a writer by night. She has
degrees from Hollins University and
Virginia Tech, and is the author of
the epic fantasy series The Creation
Saga. When not writing, she can
be found in the garden. She lives
in Southwest Virginia with the love
of her life, two excellent cats, and
a plethora of plants. You can find
out more on her website at http://
amandajmcgee.com.

The stone was smooth and clear and smoky all at once, so convincing that it looked cold to the touch. It was wrapped all around in silver so fine that it hurt Bronne's heart. She rubbed her thumb against it, hard, wishing it would shatter. Then she swung the fine chain around her neck.

Someone had to pay the cost of winter. The cost of the ice.

Alrik had taken the children away yesterday, back over the hills to their own village. They were fine children, and he was strong, and Bronne should not have been leaving them. But her village had been called upon this year to make the tithe. Reykjin was a small community, and one of the northernmost. Even so, the journey to the temple would be hard. An elder too frail could not be expected to make it, and it was not fair to ask someone too young, with life yet to live. Bronne had married late, and though her children were small they were old enough to fend for themselves, not babes in arms who still needed milk and care. That is what she told herself. If her marriage bed had become cold, if Alrik no longer touched her as he used to - well, it happened sometimes that a man wandered. It was not enough to throw her life away for, or shouldn't have been. But a priestess does not return from the ice.

She had white already in her golden hair, and her womb would birth no more children. He was young and beautiful, and yet it broke her heart all the same.

When the call came, she headed north. He came with her, to the lodge where she would be purified. It was customary for the family to come, to say their goodbyes. Then he took her children, took the light of her life imprisoned in his eyes, and left her.

Outside, she heard the women who would walk with her packing up their things. She stood, draped in blue upon blue, robes over white underclothes as thick as any she'd ever worn. It was spring here, nearing summer, but it would only get colder in the time it would take to reach their destination, no matter that the days grew longer. Such was the way of the temple. These clothes would be all that was left to her. She tried not to resent them for it.

Her companions carried flowers, and they sang. She walked among them, north, ever north.

Her own voice was silent.

***

Reykjin was one of many villages on a long spit of land between a bay and a harsh sea. Farther south, that land opened up into more verdant, temperate climes. Across the bay, impenetrable wilderness stretched. But at the tip of the peninsula, glaciers perched like shards of quartz emerging from the mountains, fading into the clouds and the cold grey ocean that seemed to stretch forever. Bronne had been there as escort, when her bosom friend Ingrid had made her own walk. Ingrid had been sick for a long time, and the women of the other villages had nearly demanded that she stay behind. Bronne had argued for her fervently. Let her death mean something. It was all Ingrid wanted.

When they had made the trek together, and Bronne had seen what became of her friend, she had not regretted it. But the loss had stayed with her.

A young girl walked with Bronne from her village, Gretta's child, Ygritte. Bronne's own mother had died in childbirth, leaving no siblings to make Bronne nieces and nephews. Her father had taken himself off to die only a spare handful of seasons ago. But the village must send someone to witness, and Gretta's girl was old enough to make the walk but not so old as to marry. There were other children to take her chores. So here she was, a pale and sullen thing. She knew the songs at least, though her voice was breathy. Not the high, lilting wail of the greatest singers, but she could carry the tune.

Bronne watched her struggle, and neither pleasure nor pity took up in her heart at the sight. She felt grief, and then rage, walking alone with only the singing for company through the scrub grass and rocks. Patches of snow could already be seen in the lees. When she noticed that, she felt fear.

The land narrowed, and the snow became thicker.

The women walking alongside her carried flowers, and the flowers did not wilt. It was a small piece of magic, of prayer. Every girl was taught the songs to keep flowers from wilting. They were old songs, older than the temple, older than the ice that sprung up about it in rippling waves and jagged crystals. Not, probably, older than the mountains, or the peninsula, though it was hard to say.

They had brought with them bricks of honeycomb, and hard

cheese, and fresh-baked bread, all saved for this occasion. They had brought cider and beer and dried fruit and nuts, and fresh vegetables and mushrooms for the first few days. No fire was lit, though all of them shivered. Fire would not do, here, in this ice, in this world beyond the seasons. No meat was eaten. That would not do either. The women carried their heavy packs, each day lighter, and sat together and took turns eating so that the songs never ceased. Their throats grew hoarse, but the flowers did not wilt and their hands did not freeze and the honey stayed soft enough to eat.

Bronne walked among them, and apart. She ate only honey and bread, at dawn. She drank only snowmelt. The songs did not warm her. The singing was ceaseless, one song bleeding into another. It lasted all through the dark of the night, when stars speckled the sky like frost. It lasted all through the morning, pink and fragile as an eggshell. It lasted all through the evening, bruised and blue as her fingers. Her heart slowed. Her steps grew heavy.

She thought of the pain of childbirth, and how it had seemed endless but had ended. The long, slow months afterward had been gray as a stormcloud, and as heavy. Even after the aching of her womb had healed, she would stand and feel surprise as the strangeness of her weight, her own weight without child, would reach to cradle a belly that wasn't there. It was the same with both Leif and Annika, though with Annika perhaps a bit easier. She'd known what to expect then, and had Leif to worry about, ricocheting around their small house with the wild abandon of a toddler who hadn't yet learned he could fall. That a fall could shatter you. Bronne would walk to the cradle, pick up the child inside, and hum to it and wish that she could have it back. Then she would drive herself to each task that needed doing, because there was no returning a baby to the belly, no keeping oneself whole when one had been split down the middle.

There was no going back.

Inch by inch, she was becoming one with the winter.

***

She felt the awareness in the ice when they were still two days from the temple. It crawled into her sleep, and gave her dreams.

The landscape had turned to white, for a time, but now color crept back in unexpectedly. The sky was bright and clear by the light of the distant sun, the cold so bitter that it should have killed her. Perhaps that is what let the thing into her dreams, that bitterness. She could feel it there, restless, wanting. Wanting something sweet to take the sting of the cold away.

Not the cold, she thought, and woke up staring into the dark sky. The stars were like needlepoints. The air cut her lungs. All around, the ice glowed, unearthly. The other women were mostly asleep now. Two lone voices braided together in the eerie darkness.

Bronne sat up and shuffled away from them. They did not follow, though she was sure their shadowed eyes watched her.

The land had narrowed, and their path had brought them close to the sea. It stretched out into the distance, and the pounding heartbeat of the waves throbbed beneath the ice that held her up. It should have been terrifying. She was too numb to be terrified.

She had made a mistake.

Surely her husband no longer loved her. Surely she was growing old, and ill with it, her heart sick with the loss of her beauty, of

147

her youth. Bronne had been tired and lonely and sad. She had cared each day for her children, and each day watched them clamber and whine for a father who would not spare her a glance or touch. All of this was true. Yet, staring over the depthless black of the ocean, Bronne longed to see Leif and Annika again, to run her fingers through their dark hair and smell the scent of them cuddled up against her. The enormity of it struck her, that she would never see them again, and that she would live for the rest of her life in regret of it.

Almost, then, she thought to end it. To throw herself into the sea and be done. She raised her foot to shuffle forward.

"Bronne?"

The sound of her name jarred her to stillness. It was not the same reaction she would have had in another place, in another time. Already the ice had its hold on her.

Gretta's girl had followed her out of the camp. She stood, wrapped in furs and shivering. Bronne turned her slow way around to look at her, at her still-pink cheeks. She remembered how Ingrid had looked, this close to the temple. She had been otherworldly, strange, and gaunt and beautiful.

Bronne did not feel beautiful, there at the edge of the bitter black sea. She felt nothing.

"Are you alright?" Ygritte asked.

Bronne found words buried deep in her chest, chipped them free.

"I dreamed of home," she said. A dream that was more than a dream. Ingrid had not cried when her dreams began to come. Bronne realized now that she could not. Tears seemed an impossibility, or perhaps the ocean and the ice were all the tears that were needed.

"Tell me about it?" Ygritte said, not quite a question. She settled herself on a rock, hunched around herself to keep warm. This far from the singing, the cold must bite and pinch her small frame.

Instead of answering her demand, Bronne said, "Have you ever been in love?"

Ygritte shook her head.

"Love is like the sea," Bronne said. "It picks you up and moves you where it wants you, and you don't have much say in that. You might stand against one wave, but not a hundred."

Bronne turned wide eyes on the horizonless dark. Wind gusted around them, and somewhere in the distance the ice moaned with it.

"I think Alrik was relieved when I left. I was just tired of standing against an ocean."

Ygritte surprised her.

"I don't think all love is like that," she said. "I think -"

Bronne waited, staring at the sea. Ygritte was shivering, still, and Bronne found herself longing to have warmth to share with her.

"When I was little," Ygritte said at last, "my grandmother became a priestess like you."

Bronne had forgotten that. She looked at her, but Ygritte had tilted her head back to look at the stars.

"Gran said that she wasn't sad to be going, because it meant that there could be flowers. She said that's why we bring flowers with us. I didn't understand it at the time. I was too little, and when you're little losing someone is just sad, nothing else. But I think love can be the way the earth holds you up. That's how Gran's love was."

Bronne was silent for a while. The wind wailed and the ocean thrummed, one singing to the other. She remembered the feeling Ygritte spoke of; it was like sunshine in winter. You could see the light, but it did not warm.

"Let's get you back to the camp," she said to Ygritte.

***

For the last days of their journey, she and Ygritte walked together. Ygritte did not sing. The flowers she carried were frosted the way Bronne was: perfectly alive, perfectly frozen. In the sunlight, ice was a tracery on her bloodless skin, yet Ygritte met her eyes unflinching.

At night, Bronne dreamed.

Her dreams were like memories. She walked through them, or was dragged through them by someone else. Awake, she knew that the presence in the dream was the ice itself. What slept there, what she now moved to serve and quiet, no one was sure of. The stories said a lot of things, but it had been a long time sleeping.

"What do you think it is?" Ygritte asked her one evening. Bronne was watching her eat. Her own body no longer hungered, but watching Ygritte brought a sparkle of memories like blown snow—fresh-baked bread and warmth and hard cheese, honey bright like golden sun on the tongue, apples and the smell of fall.

Bronne considered the question, letting the memories fade. She could feel the shape of the presence in the ice, the awareness of it that never quite left her now. Looking at it directly would be like going snowblind.

"I think it's like the stories say," Ygritte said when Bronne didn't respond. "Something large that moved through the sky. Something with scales and teeth that snapped up children." She shuddered, an exaggerated motion. She was so young.

"I don't think," Bronne said slowly, "that it eats people." She couldn't say why, exactly, except that the presence did not seem hungry. It seemed lonely instead.

She understood lonely.

As they approached the glacier that held the temple, the landscape became shatteringly beautiful. Ice hung in fluted shapes around them, the wind carving it into massive spires and odd gullies. Bronne felt the beauty move her, despite herself. Light hit the ice and turned it blue, or purple or green. At night, the stars seemed so close that they blurred with brightness, and ripples of green and pink light danced across the face of the sky. Bronne remembered this now from her prior trip, though she had forgotten it. For the first time in days, she felt her heart fill and fly with something like joy. It was almost over. That should have been scary. Instead she felt the freedom that she had been looking for when she started this long trek to her end.

"Are you afraid?" Ygritte asked her that night. Bronne shook her head. The frost in her hair crackled and flaked.

"I don't think I have any room for fear," she said.

That night, she dreamed.

Far beneath her, in the heart of the ice, a shape hung, a darker bruise on the cerulean purity of frozen water. Bronne saw it the way she saw herself - from the inside, looking at her fingers, feeling her breath. This body was massive, cool and sinuous with claws like icicles. She was coiled around herself, and, dreamily, she sensed above her tens of small lights, like warm candles. Each carried a rope, and that rope connected to her heart. Memories dropped down these ropes, a web of honey, sticky and sweet. She felt sleep, restless and eternal, miring her. Consumed dreams of the sky, drinking them down as if they might be enough to sustain her soul.

Why? Bronne asked, suddenly angry. *Why feed yourself on dreams when you should be able to reach out and grab what you want?* She thought of her husband, of his coldness. How all she had wanted, all she had longed for, was a kind word, a touch, the precious sprinklings of love.

The answer came slowly, as if from great depths. A woman, with blonde hair like Ygritte's, floated up into being. The warmth of her, the desperate love like a fire, the first chain she had wrapped around the neck of the thing below. *"So there could be flowers"* Ygritte had said, and Bronne heard this woman's memories, heard the weight of her heart. She was the anchor to the web that stretched behind her, and Bronne looked into those lights and saw dim echoes of faces, all holding the heavy, complicated weight of love.

***

When she awoke that dawn, the light stained the glacier with purples and magentas. Bronne stood, feeling the slowness of her body, her skin. The air entered her lungs sweetly.

Ygritte did not walk with her today. She sang with the rest as Bronne started out, her blue robes dusted with snow and frost. The quartz at her throat swung with her steps.

Beneath her feet, the heart of ice stirred. In the morning light, the sensation was a sharp prickling on her skin. Would it be so bad if it woke?

She remembered then the face of her distant ancestor, the first priestess. All of her sacrifice, all of the sacrifices of hundreds of other women, depended on her now. It was likely she couldn't turn back. The cold had her, after all, its magic sunk deep. But the ocean crashed nearby, steel grey. It was a final end. She understood, at last, that this sacrifice would not be.

The heart needed dreams to sustain it, and the dead did not dream.

In the end, it was not the choices of those who had come before her that moved her feet. Nor was it the companionship of those same - she understood now that she would never be alone again, and if it comforted, it was also an irony sharp as a cut. Her children crossed her mind, and her husband, but she had already made the choice to give them her death and found the choice wanting. None of these things brought her to the temple at last.

No, it was Ygritte. As they walked, she reached out her hand and took Bronne's cold fingers in her warm ones. The touch burned, but Bronne held on.

They came, singing, to the temple.

It was carved all of ice, an impossible blue bell of it that swallowed them without effort. Beneath the thin layer of its canopy, the women of the other villages sang. Their wild voices echoed eerily from the heights. The flowers in their hands glimmered with the vibrant colors of spring. Bronne let the sound wash over her, let it echo and crash inside her, undercut by the ever-present throb of the ocean.

She stood as each woman walked forward to place her flowers on an altar piled high with the offerings of all those gone before. Ygritte was the last to place her offering. She released Bronne's hand, her own hands shaking as she placed the frozen, beautiful flowers at the top. They were red against the curved columns of indigo, and Bronne felt her heart break at the color. The voices around her fell silent, at last.

Bronne looked at Ygritte, who had never been in love but knew more about it than Bronne had ever thought to.

"I wish you all the joys of spring," she said. There were tears in Ygritte's eyes. Bronne smiled.

Then she walked past the altar, and down into the depths below, to meet the thing beneath her feet.

Call To Mind

Ella Syverson

Ella Syverson is currently a student at a project based high school in northern Wisconsin, where is is able to pursue her passions: creative writing and social justice. You can find her work in Shady Grove Literary, 101 Words, Underwood Press and Silver Pen's Youth Imagination.

"Fuck! Not again," Sam curses as she steps out the driver's side door and squints down the road in the dying sunlight. Highway, grey and flat, extends through farmland and field in either direction, giving her no clue as to where she might be. *This has been happening too often lately,* she thinks, a wave of frustration and regret washing over her.

Sam shakes her head, pushing away her emotions and trying to clear the fogginess that always comes with artificial amnesia. She glances over at Diesel, grateful that at least they'd been able to keep their names. "Remember a thing?"

Diesel grimaces and rubs at his forehead. "Nope. Not since we left Jersey for the job. What's the date?"

"No idea. Dead battery." She holds up the useless phone to show him, then drops it onto the blacktop and crushes it with the heel of her boot. They would've destroyed it when she got back to HQ anyway. "You ever get sick of this gig?" She asks Diesel. They've talked about the impossibility trying to get out more times than Sam can count, but somehow she can never shake the idea.

Diesel just sighs and gets back in the car, a brand new Bentley painted a sleek, shiny silver. *I suppose our job does have a few perks,* Sam thinks, admiring the car. *They have to keep us happy somehow.* Diesel rummages around until he finds an atlas in the glovebox. At random, Sam starts driving left, looking for any sign that might let them know where they are on the map. They drive for a while in silence, but Sam is restless.

"I mean seriously. If we just kept driving, who would know?" They both recognize it's a moot point. Diesel flips on the radio, the local channel blaring classic rock.

***

It's three days later when they wind up back at HQ. Sam barely has time to sleep and shower before they're briefed on their next job. An obese man with a bushy mustache and a grey suit sits across the desk from them, puffing on a cigar. Sam coughs. She knows he's probably their boss, but can't recall ever meeting him before. She scans his desk, looking for any papers that might reveal his name, but is disappointed.

"Samantha." He sounds tired and exasperated, the kind of voice one might use with an unruly child.

"Sam," she corrects, automatically.

The fat man sighs. "Sam. Are you paying attention to me? This is an incredibly critical task. It is imperative that it is completed with all the necessary speed, stealth, and exactitude that I have come to expect from you two. Do you understand?"

Sam nods.

"Good. Let's get on with it. We have a rouge human that has gotten in with a bad crowd. So far, we know of a siren, a were-wolf, and a sorceress or witch of some kind. We'd been aware of these three for sometime, but they hadn't given us any trouble. Until now. Since we've noticed them associating with the aforementioned *human* we've lost four agents, two of which were sent in to curb the situation last week. While I would hate to lose you both, you're our best agents, so you might be the only chance we have to do this quietly. Are you willing?"

It isn't a question. "Yes, sir," Sam and Diesel say, in unison.

The fat man takes a long drag on his cigar, and then meets Sam's eyes. "Right. Exterminate all of them, including the human. Save the agents if they're still alive, and report back. If we don't hear from you in ten days, we'll send in the big guns. Understand?"

***

Two days later they're in suburbs of Chicago, sitting in the Bentley and staring at a large grey house with a neatly manicured lawn. Neither of them want to be the first to leave the car. Neither of them want to be the first to pull the trigger. It's Sam who finally gives in, slamming the car door and starting for the house without waiting for Diesel. He jogs to catch up with her. They reach the door together. Sam releases the safety on her gun, then knocks.

A wiry woman with bags under her eyes opens the door. "Hello?"

Diesel flashes his badge and Sam speaks. "We're US government agents. Let us in and we'll make this quick."

The woman opens the door a little farther, and they push their way in. Sam slams the door behind her. "What's your name?"

"Cora Martin. Agent 66215."

Sam takes a sharp breath, then tries to conceal her surprise. She'd expected the other agents to be dead. "Right. Then we're here for you. Get in the silver car across the street and we'll meet you after the job. If we're not out in ten minutes, run for it and get back to HQ."

"No," Cora answers, utterly calm. "Just stay a few minutes. We'll explain."

"Cora? Is everything all right down there?" A voice from the kitchen calls. A moment later, a tattooed man with a disgusting amount of facial hair emerges, carrying a cup of coffee. He gives Sam a toothy smile. The werewolf. She raises her gun, and is about to fire when Cora jumps in her way. Sam freezes, finger hovering on the trigger.

"Wait," Cora pleads. "Look, I'm alive and free. He hasn't killed or kidnaped anyone. He hasn't broken any DSC statutes." Still Sam keeps her gun trained on them both. What the fuck is going on? This wasn't in their briefing.

"Kill him Sam, or I will. We have orders," says Diesel from behind her. Before Sam has a chance to respond, she hears footsteps on the stairs, and glances over to see four, no five, more people hurrying into the room.

Diesel raises his gun. His hands are steady but his voice trembles. Fear? Or indecision? "U.S. Department of Supernatural Control. Which ones of you are human?"

"We won't tell you," Cora protests. "Not until you hear us out." She glances at one of the newcomers, a tall, dark skinned woman with a air of authority about her. The woman steps forward, raising her hands when Diesel snaps his gun to focus on her.

"As DSC agents," she begins, staring straight into Sam's eyes. "I'm sure you've realized that career change or retirement for that matter, isn't an option. Even with selective amnesia, we know too much. For supernatural beings, the fear of DSC extermination is ever-present. So there are some of us, an alliance of sorts, that have agreed to live in peace together. With supernatural protection and agent information on DSC, we are relatively safe. We know both of you want to join us. Actually, you already have. I'm Aliyah Jones, Agent 66198. You met me on your last job and we made a plan for you to come here. Unfortunately, you ran across a goblin lair on your last job, so they wiped you. But now you're here. You're safe."

"You're lying," Diesel growls. "What proof do we have you're not lying?"

A blue-haired girl, probably no more than sixteen, steps out from behind Aliyah. "I'm your proof. I can restore your memory."

"You're the witch," Diesel says, without lowering his gun.

"Diesel, stop," Sam says. "What if it's true?" Her mind is reeling, turning over the idea in her mind, her instinct raging against all the training she's received. Either way, they're also outnumbered. "Fine," she decides, holstering her gun. Diesel glances at her, still wary, but follows her lead. He always does. The assembled ex-agents and supernatural beings exhale a collective sigh of relief.

"Why don't you head into the kitchen and get some coffee," the blue-haired witch suggests. "I have to find the right spell on the internet. It might take a while."

Twenty minutes later, surrounded by incense and beeswax candles, the witch (they've since learned she goes by the name *Saphury*) paces in circles around them, reading what sounds like Latin from the screen of her iPhone in an increasingly dramatic tone. Sam begins to become skeptical. Is this really how magic works? And how can they be sure the spell did what Saphury said it did? Sam shifts uncomfortably on the couch cushion and stares at a candle.

The flickering orange flame dances and leaps, reminding her suddenly of—yes! That mischievous goblin! One too many family pets eaten from yards had won him a quick and early death. And there was Aliyah, too late to warn him that he was breaking DSC statutes, but just in time to return his body to the goblin colony in the abandoned New York subway tunnel. The one that the DSC allowed to remain—as long as their agents didn't find out about it. Going with Aliyah then had been their mistake, they should've waited, and ditched the burner phone with the GPS chip. At least Aliyah made it out of the car and into the woods when the Sentinel came for their memory.

Sam gasps and opens her eyes. "It's true!" She exclaims. "What do we do next?" She snatches a quick look at Diesel, and sees her own excitement mirrored in his eyes. It dulls as he considers her question.

"Boss said he'd send in the big guns if we don't show our faces back at HQ. We'll have to go back first, give a report, and book it on our next mission. Let's hope they don't wipe us."

"But they will, for sure," Sam says. "Rogue agent?" She glances at Aliyah. "They can't have us getting ideas. Maybe we can give ourselves some instructions?"

"We'll have to move base again too, right Aliyah?" says the werewolf.

"Yes. I was thinking Tampa. There's weirder shit than witches and werewolves down there." Nervous laughter. "But we'll see where we end up. Kira and Mar can shape shift, be birds or something and lead you to wherever we are when we move. Just call us when you're on your next job and we'll send them."

Sam nods. "Right. We should get going now. You're long dead."

Two weeks later, and Diesel is navigating, directing Sam to a suspected pixie den in Manhattan. "Hey Sam," Diesel says, furrowing his brow. "Check this out." Sam leans over to his seat and looks at the atlas he's holding. Between the pages is a sheet of notebook paper with a letter addressed to them. As she reads the letter, Sam feels a growing sense of—what is it, exactly? Not happiness, not relief, not even excitement... hope, maybe. If everything in this note is true, and if they can pull it off, she'd never have to kill again. She'd be done taking orders. She'd have her mind back. She'd be free. "So..." Diesel asks.

"So we'll need a new phone." Sam makes a sharp right, taking the nearest exit and cruising through lots of strip malls until they reach the nearest Best Buy.

Ten minutes later they're heading back to the Bentley. As they approach it, a pair of crows alight on the hood of the car, appraising them with beady black eyes. One of them gives a loud squawk, then they both take to the air and begin to fly towards the highway. Sam and Diesel watch the crows disappear, jump into the car, and glance at each other, both of them grinning with anticipation. Sam puts her foot the gas and starts driving south.

Sirens

Britani C.W. Baker

Britani is a PhD candidate in Literature at the University of Southern Mississippi where she studies 19th Century American Literature and Utopia/Dystopia. Her fiction has previously appeared in Product Magazine.

Isaac says she's weird. Denver doesn't like that word—weird. When she thinks of Isaac she thinks of the stars. That's why she likes him so much. Denver tells him there once was someone named Isaac Newton who proved the sun was the center of the solar system by calculating the trajectories of comets. He tells her that's a coincidence. She tells him it's not. Circles are never coincidences.

She doesn't think Isaac really likes her all that much. Stars may be easy, but faces are hard. When Denver tells Isaac about the synchronicity of the universe he asks her where she learns words like synchronicity. Denver tells him that she reads them, but he doesn't believe her. He asks her to read things sometimes and she can't do it. Reading isn't like that. The letters get jumbled. Reading is the same as circles. You have to really work at circles. Usually perfect circles just happen, and you don't actually make them happen. That's what reading's like.

Isaac found her in an old house about a year ago. She was seven when the tornadoes hit. Denver doesn't really remember much before. Just a bunch of sound and noise. Isaac tells her that the tornadoes happened everywhere, things didn't always used to look like this. He says that for a while people tried to fix things, but within weeks the money just ran out, no one had any supplies. The sirens never stopped going off. She doesn't think he really understands it all.

They're scavenging. Isaac tells her that she has to learn not to be a crybaby. The sirens hurt her ears, and she wants to go back to the silo. Denver's only nine, but Isaac says that he was scavenging when he was ten, and he wasn't such a crybaby.

"Can we stop soon?" she asks.

"Let's just get to the silo."

"But I'm tired. My feet hurt."

He sighs. "Ok. We can stop for ten minutes. But then we're going to the silo. We have more work to do tomorrow."

They stop next to a milk truck. Isaac takes off his backpack, pulls out a water and hands it to Denver. She takes it without looking in his eyes. Eye contact makes her uncomfortable. The sirens continue to blare. Isaac looks at his watch, a relic from before the tornadoes hit. Denver keeps rubbing her foot in the dirt in a circle. She makes circles a lot. At night sometimes Isaac watches her move her feet in circular motions when she's trying to sleep. Isaac doesn't know that she sees him watching. It comforts her, calms her down. It's because of the stars. She pictures the galaxy as one big circle, the planets revolving around the sun, the moon revolving around the earth, everything ineffable, unbroken.

It's been fifteen minutes and Isaac tells her they have to go. They pick up their bags and start walking.

***

Denver doesn't want to go out today. She has a bad feeling about the whole thing. But Isaac says they didn't find enough yesterday.

Just some old towels, an expired can of ravioli, and some empty water bottles. She looks at the house that Isaac says they're going to search and hopes that they can't find a way in.

The sirens are not quite as loud here but they're still loud enough to hurt. The noise pitches up and down, up and down, a circle that never stops. Even at the silo you can faintly hear the circular scream of the sirens from the city.

When they get inside the house there's trash everywhere. She doubts they'll find anything. Broken table, broken chairs, broken fireplace, broken stairway, broken cabinet. A layer of dust and dirt covers everything, making it hard to breathe. Denver covers her nose and mouth with her shirt.

"Take shallow breaths and start looking around."

She follows Isaac's orders and begins searching. She opens cabinets whose doors are barely hanging on, digs through piles of rubble. The house groans.

As she searches, Denver thinks about Isaac's horses. Isaac used to have horses at the farm. There's just the silo left now. Isaac thinks his parents are going to come back to the silo. That's why he doesn't want to leave. He said they used to have all types of animals she's never seen. He won't talk about his parents, but sometimes he'll talk about the animals. Denver imagines feeding a horse an apple, it breathing in her face, feeling its energy pulsing into her. She runs her hands along a dirt-covered armoire like she's stroking a horse's muzzle. Denver mirrors the hand motions she's seen Isaac make when he gets caught up in his story and pretends he's stroking a horse, too. She imagines what it was like for Isaac before the tornadoes. What it was like to have parents. Isaac carries a picture of his parents with him, but he's never shown it to her. Denver took it from his pocket when he was sleeping once. His mom had the same curly brown hair as him. His dad's eyes had those little wrinkles near the corners.

Denver searches through a pile on the floor. There's ripped clothes, too dirty and tattered to be useful, a broken lamp, some pieces of unidentifiable metal, and a stuffed gorilla. The gorilla's missing an eye. She drops it back on the pile. Something shifts under Denver's foot, and the floor groans.

"Isaac?" He's in a different room and doesn't come immediately.

"Isaac?" Her voice rises an octave. Denver sees a snake squirm underneath a nearby ceiling beam.

Isaac runs in, nearly tripping over the leg of a broken chair. "Denver? What's wrong?"

"Listen."

He stands still. They can hear the usual house sounds. But they can hear other things too. Denver can hear the sound of Isaac breathing. She can hear the sound of her heart, blood throbbing in her ears.

The sirens had stopped. Isaac runs outside; Denver follows. He looks up and down the street, up at the sky.

She hears a faint clicking sound and realizes it's Isaac flicking his fingernails together. For the first time, the circle has stopped. In a silence that isn't silent they walk outside, neither of them knowing what to say. They stand there for a while not talking, listening. Denver's feet scuffle on the ground as she shifts. Sounds assault her. Like the sirens before. There are so many sounds. But these aren't circular. These are memories. A small, dark room. The sound of her breathing. Every noise magnified.

Isaac speaks, and she jumps. "Come on. We have to keep searching."

"Can't we go back to the silo?"

"We haven't even found anything."

The silence is worse than the sirens.

"But the sirens."

"It doesn't mean anything, ok?" Isaac kicks a piece of wood on the ground, his mouth turning down into a frown.

They walk back into the house to grab their bags, each step scraping, dragging, scratching. Denver lifts her feet more carefully. Straight up, forward, down. Don't drag. Don't scrape. But Isaac's footsteps reverberate in her head. Denver places her hands over her ears. Tears gather in her eyes.

Isaac looks at her, questioning. She can feel it in his gaze, thinking it - weird.

In space it's quiet. Complete silence. Sound doesn't travel in a vacuum. Even though not all of space is a vacuum. Humans just can't perceive the sound traveling through the dense molecular clouds of gases left over from star formation. It can take anywhere from 100,000 to 10 million years for a star to form.

Isaac stops; Denver almost runs into him. He turns, grabs her and begins dragging her back towards the house. Denver lets out a small shriek before he clamps his hand over her mouth.

"Shhhhh. Quiet. People are coming."

Voices. A man and a woman, moving towards them, getting louder.

Inside the house Isaac pushes her behind a fallen dresser. "Don't move. Keep quiet."

Denver clamps her hand over her mouth and nose so that she doesn't breathe dust and sneeze. It's dark, cramped. Her breath sounds louder than it should. She tries to take shallower breaths but she feels suffocated. Feels trapped. She knows Isaac told her not to move, but she has to get out. She crawls out from behind the dresser, her hands scraping along the wooden floors. She pauses, hears muffled voices.

"Isaac?" she whispers.

"Denver. What are you doing?" A whisper from her right. She sees him near the wall, peeking through a crack. He has his pocket knife in one hand, a gift from his dad years ago. She crawls towards him. She tries to be quiet, but her leg knocks over a side table barely standing from mold and decay.

"What was that?" The man speaking.

"They're coming."

They hear footsteps on the porch. Isaac stands and grabs Denver. "Come on."

There's only one way out. The door is blocked by debris. They came in through a hole in the wall where a tree had fallen. Isaac has told her about the bad people before. He says that until the adults come back they have to be extra careful. The silo is far enough out that they don't often get people coming through. But Isaac says he has heard people at night sometimes. She's told Isaac that there aren't really any bad people, that St. Augustine said all of nature is good since the Creator of all of nature is supremely good. That while the good in a thing can be diminished and that debasement is evil, the good can never disappear completely. So, everyone contains good in them. There are no bad people.

Isaac grips his knife and they run towards the exit. They reach the hole in the wall and round the corner. A hand grabs Denver's arm. Callused, large. Isaac lunges towards the man, knife outstretched. The man pushes Denver to the ground and grabs Isaac's wrist, twisting. Isaac drops the knife. He bends Isaac's arm behind him. Denver pushes herself up onto her hands and knees, her hands scraped and bleeding. Isaac's knife is on the ground, not far away. She crawls towards the knife. Before she can grab it, a hand wraps around her leg, pulls her back. She yells and kicks out, looks over at Isaac who is on the ground while the man holds a gun on him.

"Shut her up, Anne."

"She won't stop moving." Anne's breath reeks.

The woman drags Denver towards Isaac. Isaac seems dazed.

She pushes Denver to the ground. Denver catches herself and crawls towards Isaac. He doesn't speak.

Denver remembers a woman, her mother, who used to push her. She remembers darkness and yelling. Her mother was always angry.

They're watching Denver and Isaac as ifsizing them up to see if they're worth anything. Anne's hair is knotted. The man looks like he hasn't showered in far too long and hasn't taken any strides towards hygiene.

"Who you got with you?" the man asks.

Anne looks around nervously.

Denver looks at Isaac. He's still dazed. Looks like he's going to have a black eye where the man hit him.

"Our parents," Denver answers him, a small voice. She wishes Isaac could answer.

"Yeah? Where're they at then?"

"They...they went to search the house down the street. The one with...with the blue shutters." She stutters. Doesn't make eye contact.

They look down the street in the direction Denver points.

"Go look," he says to Anne.

"I'm not going to look. It'd be two on one. Don't know what kind of weapons they got," Anne says. "You're the one with the gun. You go."

He glares at her, eyebrows sinking. "The little freak is probably lying anyways. Their parents aren't with them."

Denver's back in the dark room. Her mother yelling at her. Freak. Her fists clench.

"Well if that's what you think, give me the gun and go look." Anne holds out her hand.

While they are arguing, the man drops his gun. Denver reaches behind Isaac and grabs a jagged length of metal lying on the ground. It's heavier than she thought. She bumps Isaac, but he doesn't move.

The man sees her moving and refocuses on Denver. "What're you doing?"

He picks up the gun. She lunges. Denver's slower than normal, the piece of metal heavy in her hands. She aims for the man's knees. He pulls the trigger as the metal jabs his right shin. The bullet splinters the ground near Isaac.

The sound is so loud it echoes. Denver has never heard something so loud before. It's louder than the sirens. She covers her ears, screaming.

Cursing, the man grabs the metal slat and throws it.

"What the fuck do you think you're doing?" He points the gun at Denver. She crawls backwards, crab-like, trying to get away.

"Let's just take their stuff and go," Anne says.

"Little shits. We should just kill them."

"What about their parents?"

"If their parents are with them then why haven't they come? Must've heard the girl's screaming before."

"Well they're probably coming now since you shot the gun. Fuckwit." The last word is whispered, barely audible.

"What'd you call me?"

Denver reaches over and pulls the picture out of Isaac's pocket. Isaac grabs her hand, gaining awareness. She yanks away.

"Stop moving. What's wrong with you?" the man yells.

She holds it out to him. He grabs it.

"Those are our parents. They're going to kill you when they get here." She doesn't look him in the eyes, but her voice is cold, steady.

"Come on, Jim. Let's just go. Really, they're not worth it. They're just kids. We can take their stuff and go. If their parents are with them, then they could be here any minute. Let's go. Head towards Baltimore. There ain't nothing left here."

"I told you, we ain't going to Baltimore."

"We don't got time for this Jim." Anne glances down the street.

Jim looks at Anne, considering. He drops the pictures of Isaac's parents on the ground, stepping on it.

"Fine. Grab their bags."

She searches through Denver's pockets. Nothing there. Searches through Isaac's pockets and finds a box of matches. Anne shoves the matches in her pocket.

"That's it. Let's go." The man shifts the gun, putting it by his side. He glances at them one last time. They grab the bags and run.

Denver picks up Isaac's crumpled picture and shuffles towards him.

"Isaac? You ok?"

She holds out the picture and he reaches to take it.

"Just a headache."

"They took all our stuff."

He pauses. A beat too long. "It's going to be ok."

Isaac always says that.

**

They walk in the opposite direction the man and woman went.

Heading farther into the city. Isaac says they have to keep searching. Denver protests, says he needs to rest, but he says he's fine. They need to get supplies, he says.

Silent, they listen to the sounds around them. Something flutters to Denver's left. A creak to her right. In the distance, more birds. The city has been overrun with birds since the tornadoes hit, every broken building full of nooks and crannies for birds to nest in. They hear more voices in the distance, but can't tell which way they come from. Sounds echo. Their footsteps resound on the pavement. Isaac tells Denver to try to walk on the weedy parts to soften their footfalls. They don't want to attract attention. They have to go farther into the city than usual to find buildings they haven't already rummaged through. Supplies are getting harder and harder to find.

Denver worries that they should move away from the silo, but Isaac refuses.

They pass a hospital that was left mostly intact after the tornadoes. Isaac says they can't go in the larger buildings. There's too much chance that the whole thing could topple down on top of them and they wouldn't be able to dig their way out. It's safer to stick to the smaller houses and low-lying buildings. Other people are also less likely to have scavenged the smaller houses, skipping over them for the big buildings, thinking big buildings equal more supplies. Also, the hospital probably has squatters.

They try to stick to the sides of buildings as much as possible, stay in the shadows, just in case. Around one building it looks like someone set up walls. Jagged pieces of metal and wood from torn down buildings stick in the air. There are holes in the makeshift walls, like it hasn't been kept up in a while. Probably no one stays there anymore.

It starts to rain. Denver can hear the patter of rain on the pavement. Soft at first then louder. Too loud. They are near what used to be a sandwich shop. The sign above the door reads "Sam's Sandwiches." Or used to, some letters are missing. It's not ideal, but Isaac says they can't risk getting sick in the rain.

"Come on. In here." Isaac pulls Denver towards the shop.

When they get inside, Isaac heads towards the back. Denver follows. He wants them to get out of sight of the broken windows. Chairs are knocked over. In the kitchen, pots, pans, and silverware are scattered everywhere. There are still some cups and plates on the tables, but the place has definitely been scavenged already. All the food that would keep is probably long gone. Denver tries to avoid stepping on things, so the sound doesn't hurt her ears, each vibration jarring. Isaac stuffs a pot and pan in his bag. They have a few back at the silo already, but a couple more couldn't hurt. Denver walks around, trying to avoid making noise. She carefully digs through a pile of opened cans near the fridge. One can's label says "sweet corn." She's not sure if she's ever had sweet corn, tries to imagine what it would taste like. She keeps digging. Denver finds a lighter that doesn't work, a book with most of the pages missing, and a half-melted candle. She grabs the book and candle and stuffs them in her bag. The place hasn't only been scavenged, someone had apparently been squatting.

Denver looks over at Isaac. He opens a freezer door and a rank stench hits them. Denver covers her nose, gags. Isaac quickly shoves the door closed. He looks at Denver. "Sorry. Food's gone bad."

Returning to her search, Denver sees a piece of paper in a small space between the fridge and the cabinet. She reaches over and grabs it. It's a photograph. Just like the one Isaac carries. In the photo, a girl sits on her dad's shoulders. She smiles, grabbing onto his hair. They are at the ocean. You can see the water shining behind them and other people walking around.

The man looks familiar. Or maybe it's the girl who looks familiar.

No. It's the ocean.

There was an ocean over their fireplace. The house was always dark. The picture was dark. Not like this picture, sunny and happy. The picture over their fireplace was stormy. Like a hurricane was about to hit. The waves were choppy, harsh. She never knew the ocean could look so bright.

"Denver, you ok? Did you find anything?" His eyes linger on the paper in her hand.

"The ocean's tide is caused by the gravitational pull of the moon."

"What?"

She hears Isaac coming towards her, but she doesn't turn. He seems far away. She's back in that dark house. The dark room. A closet. A woman, her mother, calling her a freak. *Children shouldn't know what you know.* Hitting her. *Children should listen, not speak.* Pushing her. *I wish you had never been born.* Trapped for hours. Everything quiet. She's hyperventilating. Her breath is too loud. She shifts position and it's too loud. She can't see anything. Feeling the walls around her, she curls into the corner. She cries for her mother. She wants to get out. After a while, drawing circles on the floor, Denver begins to calm down. The repetition slowing her heart. She rubs her feet together in a circular motion. When she wakes up there's a loud sound. It's everywhere. She covers her ears. A crack runs up the door, splitting the door in two. Through the crack nothing but darkness. She can see things flying around. A chair spins circles in the air. Within seconds everything is over. The sound recedes. Still loud, but getting quieter. Eventually all

Denver hears is a siren. Up and down. Over and over. Never stopping. She pushes open the door and the house is gone. She can see the sky, and the stars open up before her.

"Denver?" Isaac's voice is panicked. He grabs her shoulder, but she yanks away.

"Don't touch me."

"Denver? What's wrong? What is it?"

She feels angry. Angrier than she's ever felt. She pushes him. Denver runs out of the kitchen, back towards the broken glass windows in the shop front, picture still in hand. She hears Isaac following her but doesn't stop. She picks up a chair and throws it through what remains of the window. Glass shatters. The sound is loud. It hurts, but she doesn't care.

"Denver—!"

She grabs a piece of wood, a broken table leg, and hits anything that will break. Ceramic cups and plates left on tables, a cracked mirror.

Isaac watches, unable to stop her, not knowing what to do.

Eventually the swinging begins to slow. The crashes become further apart. Denver sinks to the floor. She sees Isaac across the room staring at her, and her anger rekindles. "Stop looking at me like I'm weird!" she shouts.

Isaac doesn't respond. He stands there staring at Denver, at the anger on her face. He sees the picture on the floor where she dropped it, and unconsciously gropes in his pocket for his own.

He walks over to where Denver sits and grabs the table leg out of her hand. He turns and walks to one of the windows that Denver hadn't thrown a chair through. There is a giant hole in the middle of the glass, like someone had chucked a rock at it. Isaac raises the table leg like a bat, and swings. He turns to the room and smashes every cup and plate that Denver missed. Shards of ceramic hit the wall. For once, he doesn't seem to care about making too much noise. He drops the table leg, picks up a chair and smashes it over and over on the floor until it breaks. He's screaming, Denver doesn't know what. Just some unintelligible sounds.

Denver watches him.

When he finishes, Isaac falls to the floor next to Denver, breathing heavily.

Sometimes Denver wishes she was in the stars. Floating high above everyone. Looking down on the earth. The change of pressure in space would rupture her lungs, make her implode; her skin would swell as the water in her body began to vaporize, and she would become just another piece of the universe.

They sit there, each consumed in their own memories.

"It's stopped raining," Isaac says.

Denver looks outside and it's dark. The storm clouds still hang overhead, but the rain has stopped.

She looks over and Isaac is making circles. He runs his finger in a circle, over and over on the floor.

He reaches across her and grabs the picture she dropped. Isaac looks at it, the father and daughter at the ocean. He turns to Denver.

Digging around in his head for a fact, any fact, something about the water, ... "You know, the ocean has over 20,000 kinds of fish."

He puts the picture in his pocket, next to the one of his parents.

Green is for Wishes and Apples

Kathryn McMahon

Kathryn McMahon is a queer American writer living abroad with her British wife and dog. Her fiction has appeared or is forthcoming in places such as PodCastle, Syntax and Salt, and in the food and horror anthology Sharp & Sugar Tooth: Women Up to No Good (Upper Rubber Boot, 2019). On Twitter, she is @ katoscope. Find more of her writing at darkandsparklystories.com.

Branches sag under the weight of Granny Smiths that gleam like giant emeralds. Abigail reaches for a fruit, sliding her sneakers up the trunk, twists an apple free, and bites in. But unripe, it's too sour. She lets it slip from her fingers and plunge through the leaves. She should know better, but it's hard *not* to eat them when she remembers how delicious they can be. That, and the apples are lush with power. The crisp green of Granny Smiths is perfect for life magic. The energy in red apples is too often misunderstood by the more impatient magics of death and love. That's why fairy tales favor them. Abigail rubs the gnarled bark, and the green apples bob in encouragement. Though she knows it depends on who uses apples and what they're used for, she's never heard of them bringing back the dead. But if she can carve an apple doll, carve a face so true to life it'll be a portrait in fruity flesh, will that bring back her grandmother?

She tries to ignore the guilt that knots around her heart. Gram was sick. It can't be her fault she's dead. It can't.

A breeze, the first earthy breath of autumn decay, snakes out from the cedar forest and rattles the leaves around her. If she's learned anything about magic, it's that the apple tree will need something in exchange if it's to concentrate its wonders in a form *she* can use. Maybe it wants a few drops of her blood? Abigail climbs down and, as if in answer, a twig scrapes her arm and takes the blood for itself. At least she doesn't have to worry about pricking her finger.

She wanders through the orchard inspecting apple trees for rust or blight. Double-checking that no others call to her before she loses something else she can't get back. None do. Out of the dozens of trees, there is only that one, that special one. It's the one she has sat under most, reading or thinking or drawing. It's the one she can see from her window as it rises above the others. It's not really a surprise that it calls to her. Or that it's a little larger than the rest. It is, after all, the tree around which her family is buried.

A few years ago, driving up the interstate to visit her grandmother for the long weekend, her dad swerved to avoid a deer and sent their car careening into an oak. Abigail doesn't remember the accident, but she's the only one who survived. She had nowhere else to go but Gram's. They ate a lot of venison that first week. Her grandmother said it was payback, but at the time Abigail didn't really think about what that might have meant. She just burrowed into Gram's lap and cried and cried while Gram stroked her hair.

Abigail needed toys, Gram said, so she taught her how to make apple dolls. They carved and dried a father, two older brothers, a mother—a whole family of leathery, withered faces to replace the ones they'd lost.

But those dolls were just *dolls*. It hasn't been long since Abigail played with them—it hasn't been long since Gram's last breath, either. The memory catches in her throat like a seed.

She returns to her tree as the sun sinks towards the jagged jaw of sky. Out from the cedars darts a raccoon, its eyes putrid, its coat almost bare. On its hind leg rises the knotted ridge of scars left by a trap's metal teeth.

Abigail might not recall the car accident, but the funeral she remembers. It was spring. The apple trees were blooming and it looked like snow had caught in their leaves. Then a breeze came and shook the petals into all four graves. Gram had said she wanted her family close to home, not in a cemetery surrounded by strangers. Only eight, Abigail had been too little to dig the graves while her grandmother was too arthritic—and too broke to hire anyone. But when Abigail helped roll her mother into the ground, she saw how the dirt walls had been scraped by claws.

They belonged to one more secret, rescued thing. As for the raccoon stalking her? She'd watched Gram padding herbs inside the dead animal's wounds before stitching them up, then saw her lay its body on the porch steps under the moon. Somehow Gram had known Abigail was spying and spoke without turning around. "One more thing to keep the house safe," was all she'd said.

Anger rushes through her. When she'd realized what Gram could do, she'd asked her to give the apple dolls life, to give her family back to her, but Gram refused. She said they wouldn't be the same. There wasn't enough of them left.

At least now she can't stop me, thinks Abigail. And she hopes, too, that she has spied enough, gleaned enough from her grandmother to know what she's doing.

Somewhere in the orchard, the raccoon is watching her. She can feel it. She heads to the cottage and from the mantel fetches the cookie tin heavy with ashes. It was only a few days ago that she'd swept Gram's charred remains out of the fire. It had taken hours for her to burn—and most of the wood stored for winter. But she can always chop more. Though tears ran down her cheeks and into the flames and, later, into the dust, she was not about to waste Gram on worms and beetles and other things waiting hungrily in the earth.

Abigail carries the ashes to the tree, and when she opens the tin, the perfume of smoke circles her as if the fire is right *there*. Fresh.

In her periphery, she catches her oldest brother's face flashing across the shiny skin of an apple. But she has no use for warnings. She sprinkles soot and bits of blackened bone over the roots. Puts Gram into the fruit. Foolishly, she'd waited too long in bloodletting and the fluid had become tacky and congealed. With the ashes, her fingertips come away gray and itching, and she wipes them on her jeans.

There on the moss lies the apple with her bite stolen from its hard, green shell. She picks it up and nibbles it again. Yes, *much* too sour. The sky is ripe with sunset and, hanging above her clapboard cottage, the moon is a single white feather. By the time it is full and round as an old, dimpled face, the apples will have sweetened. Maybe they'll restore a sweetness to Gram's nature. And a forgiveness. Abigail misses having her hair stroked.

She tosses the apple into the orchard. Where it falls with a thud, the raccoon dashes out and snatches it in its bony paws before disappearing again into the forest.

When her apple dolls eventually spoiled, she'd found that dead raccoon looting their moldy heads from the compost. "Death attracts death," said Gram when she told her. But death attracts hope, too.

A cloud passes over the moon. She'll watch the sky and wait.

***

Down the road at the farmers' market, Abigail sells jars of raw honey and bunches of dried herbs and doesn't bother to remember the tourist faces that change every day. She's been coming here since she was little. Every summer, every weekend. After the first week with her grandmother, things settled into a new normal. On top of homeschooling, she learned how to harvest and dry rosemary, how to make jam from blackberries, collect honey from bees, haul it all to the farmers' market, and tie ribbons on everything, just so, for the tourists to buy.

She also learned how to keep from crying in front of them—even when they bought apple dolls, plain-faced and anonymous. The strangers cooed over how cute and quaint everything was here in the back of beyond. And Abigail learned to nod and smile.

Now, it's hard to remember how. What will the new normal be? What will it be like having Gram back, a little apple doll stuffed in her backpack making sure she's talking up her wares?

A tiny voice pops up inside her. What if—what if she comes back mad? Abigail pushes it down. No. She'll come back and all will be forgiven.

Old Mrs. Crockett shuffles over from her fruit stall. "It's so strange seeing you here without Dot. Where is the old girl?"

"Oh, Gram is off visiting family." In a way, she is.

Mrs. Crockett frowns in surprise, but at least she lets her be, and Abigail trades some herbs for one of her lemons. She'll need it to prepare the apple doll. She holds the fruit away from her like a small, hard star about to explode.

Every night, she goes home and sits by her apple tree. She presses her hands to its rough bark. She hugs tight its ugly branches. Wishing. Pleading. Trying to breathe normally as that guilty little knot around her heart grows tighter. Tighter.

She used to dream about her parents and brothers, Nick and George. They wore ancient apple peels instead of skin and smelled of pie when they played with her. Now she dreams and sees an old woman with an apple face humming lullabies as she sits on her rocker and knits. But the needle slips and pierces her thumb. Out flows juice, and the old woman begins to moan.

Abigail wakes shivering.

Something is scratching at the window. There are no trees or bushes near enough for that to be it. She hopes it's only the raccoon.

The scratching won't stop. She peers out. It's too dark to see much, but nosing above the trees is a full moon of clotted cream.

Her stomach clenches. It's time to harvest the apples. She knows this deep inside herself in a way that Gram always talked about as *bone-knowing*.

Abigail pulls on a sweatshirt, slips her feet into sneakers, and grabs a flashlight and a sack from the cupboard. Earlier that evening— or was it yesterday?—she thought to cut up another sack, sew it, and fill its belly and limbs with split peas. She jammed in a dowel for a spine and made a dress from Gram's faded floral apron. The doll waits, headless, in the kitchen. She needs one last thing: the perfect apple. She steps out into the night in search of it.

She has been so excited, so impatient, but her fingers are trembling. What if none of them are good enough? She clutches the burlap tighter.

On nights like this, she knows she isn't the only one drawn to the energy pulsing in the orchard. Batwings whisper past her and things rustle above in the branches. A half-dead squirrel? A robin with one, bony wing? Under the leaves, it's too dark to spot them. Abigail has left lamps on in the cottage and they glow, watching as she feels her way among the apple trees. But she is not so afraid of the night or its secrets. She has grown up alongside them. Maybe, just maybe, she *is* one.

The branches bow like her grandmother's back and the fruit is heavy and tart. She doesn't need to taste it to know. The apples smell ripe against the cold, dank autumn air crackling in her lungs. Somewhere to the east, one of her neighbors has built a wood fire. It, too, is drawn to the magic, and smoke circles the tree in a gently swirling haze faintly lighter than the pitch of night.

From her pocket, Abigail takes her small flashlight and flicks it on. Its beam is as cold as moonlight, but denser, and as she shines it over the apples, they seem to retreat from its stare. She understands. She, too, prefers the shadows.

She clenches the flashlight in her teeth and shakes open her sack. There's no need to climb; the apples hang low. As she reaches for them, fallen leaves make a roving skirt around her jeans and flutter hungrily for the energy she collects in the burlap. She nests the apples gently so they don't bruise.

There are enough for dozens of dolls' heads, but she will make only one. And the rest? The tourists wouldn't want these—or she doesn't *want* them to want these. Bits of Gram and Mom and Dad, elements of Nick and George. They belong to her. She will brew apple cider. Stew apple butter. Bake apple pies. Her grandmother will wake to an apple feast.

Abigail has always shared meals with her dolls. Crumbs of crusty rolls and cheese. Mugs of milk. Cobblers of wild blueberries or peaches. Her old apple dolls never touched these, of course, but it was good to pretend.

She stops, apple in hand. Will Gram be able to taste such things once she comes back? Will she enjoy them on her own apple tongue?

So Abigail fills the sack with fruit for herself and in falls another morsel of worry. In the cedar grove, a pair of barn owls talk, their faces like ghosts.

Back in the cottage, she locks the door with its iron key and pulls the gingham curtains shut. No one is around to see in, but it doesn't hurt to be too careful when things get restless, jealous, even hungry if they sniff magic nearby.

She builds a log fire and sets a small pot of water and forest herbs to boil above it. If she is lucky, the odor of wild leek and wild rocket will cloak the scent of a magic apple drying in the oven.

In the kitchen, she picks up the lemon from the market. It is precious, traded for more than a few bundles of thyme and sage. She raises it to her lips and kisses it lightly as if it will turn her hopes to truth. Sunny hints of citrus dance under her nose, and as she slices the lemon, a kind of clean washes over her. For a moment, she feels cut loose of guilt. But that moment doesn't last. She squeezes the juice into a bowl of water and, whispering her own spontaneous incantation, sprinkles sea salt in a circle above it. Then she turns on the oven and drags over a stool and the sack of apples. Lining them up in a row on the counter, she selects the one with the clearest skin and roundest shape, though neither will matter once she starts cutting.

Out of the corner of her eye, Dad's face flickers over an apple sitting on the counter. She looks away before she sees something she doesn't want to.

The headless doll leans against a jar of homemade pickles. Its apron-turned-dress is wrinkled—Gram won't appreciate that—but it's the least of Abigail's worries. The doll droops to one side almost impatiently, and fear whirls through her. What if she doesn't get this recipe right? These apples are a little larger than most. What if it's too heavy and her grandmother can't raise her head, like when she was in bed, ill and hot with fever? What if—what if Abigail gets it wrong and nothing happens?

Guilt crowds out her breath.

She should've handled things differently when Gram was sick. *A lot* differently. Gotten help sooner. Gotten any at all.

Abigail picks up her paring knife, hands shaking. She pushes away nerves—and the guilt that has tied itself around *all* of her organs—and skims the blade over the apple. As she peels, a bright vine unwinds to her knees.

There's another scratch at the window. Is it the raccoon? An owl? Something else? She ignores it, but that doesn't stop the tingle that zips down her back. The kitchen fills with a stewed, peppered pungency from the pot of boiling herbs—and the scratching stops.

The bare apple is smooth and sticky-fleshed. Holding the stem, she dips it in the lemon water to soak as she eats up the green, snapping skin and wipes juice from her lips. She doesn't take her eyes off the peeled apple.

When she and Gram had sewed dolls' clothes from would-be quilt scraps, Abigail, new to needlework, pricked her finger more than once. Each time, Gram clucked and carefully wiped away the blood, making sure the bright red never touched anything that might go near the green apples. There is always danger in making a doll. So many things can go wrong. Not only to fingers. Cut too deep, and the apple will rot. Don't dry it long enough, and the apple will rot. Sometimes, they just want to go bad. Eventually, doesn't everything?

As her family of apple dolls began to spoil, she'd wanted to cook and eat the beans inside them. Carry part of her family within her, never mind that it wasn't real. She thought Gram had indulged her when she made ham and bean soup one night, but after dinner when Abigail was scraping the pot, she'd found a mound of worm-threaded navy beans amid the apple faces molding in the compost. She took an old bean and swallowed it. It was soft and foul, and later, though her stomach twisted and spasmed, she'd had no regrets. The next morning, she went back for more beans and that's when she discovered the dead raccoon holding George's moldy face in its jaws. It hissed, scaring her off.

There are dead things and then there are *dead* things. She's very glad indeed that Gram never had to reanimate her—if she even would have. She doesn't want to think about what her family would look like if Gram had stuffed and stitched up their bodies. They wouldn't be able to go anywhere, do anything, without drawing unwanted attention.

But a little apple doll hidden in a backpack? That's different.

"Come on, Gram. Come back," says Abigail, plucking the peeled apple from the lemon water and dabbing it with a rag. Thumbing her paring knife, she begins to carve. An ear here, its lobe stretched as if by a silver hoop. Another there. Cheekbones to capture dark eyes, of course. A nose that will pinch as it dries. And what else but a tiny chin and smile? She hopes her grandmother will remember how to smile.

She inspects the fruit. It's Gram's face—but younger. Livelier. She ties twine to its stem and hangs it inside of the oven where it will wrinkle-dry. Though the fire has died to glowing coals, the pot continues to bubble. Perhaps it is the ashy trace of Gram among the brickwork that keeps it simmering. And even with the boiling herbs, Abigail can smell the magic in the room—like damp fur and lilac.

It's either very late or very early, she doesn't care which. Yawning, she pulls the faded quilt from Gram's rocker and goes to sit on the stool by the oven. She keeps the lip of the door open to warm herself with its hot, apple sighs and falls asleep at the counter, head on hands, the row of rejected apples bumping away. In her dream, blossoms drip tears, not rain, and whisper. Whisper.

Abigail wakes to the sound of screaming. It's coming from the oven, its door still ajar.

She snips the twine and, with the edge of the quilt, draws out the warm, dried apple. The heat has withered it, and it glares with her grandmother's cracked, old face and does not stop screaming.

She knows that scream. As Gram's bones ate themselves up and her skin mottled with sores, Abigail could do nothing to help. But she'd tried. She foraged for feverfew and other herbs. For mushrooms. She plucked and boiled chickens and poured the broth down Gram's throat. Anything to stop that screaming. For days, neither slept, until at last Abigail took her grandmother's pillow and buried the old woman's face.

She should've gotten a neighbor. Called an ambulance. Chased down a doctor—one of many among the tourists, or so she assumed. But who would've wanted to come back here to a falling down cottage visited by dead animals and dotted with family graves? They would've called social services. Like they did before, after the car accident.

Now, cradled in the blanket, apple eyes tightly shut, Gram's mouth breaks into a sweet, hollow O of anguish. Part of her has seeped into the fruit. The very worst part.

It's too much. Abigail cannot fix this. What can she do to end the screaming?

The kitchen window squeaks open and bony paws part the curtains. The dead raccoon has found a way in.

It hops towards her, its knuckles scraping the oak floorboards. The circles on its tail are all but smoke rings. Though its fur is thinning, it still wears a black mask around what remains of its eyes.

The apple, propelled by moans, sways on the stem between Abigail's fingers. She tries to steady it as the raccoon raises scabby paws to her.

One more thing to keep the house safe, Gram had said.

Abigail's chest tightens. *Did she mean safe from me?*

She'd wanted to hold onto some essence of her grandmother, of her family, and now what can she do? She bends to give the raccoon the apple head.

The curtains twitch with a breeze creeping in from the night—the night that she is only afraid of in the same way in which she is afraid of herself.

Her apple is just above the raccoon's skeletal fingers when she pauses.

The screaming doesn't.

The raccoon drops its paws as Abigail lifts the apple to her own lips, parts her teeth—and bites in.

Laughter in the Graveyard

Mab Morris

Mab Morris has published three books in fantasy and fantasy-mystery. She is becoming known for her world building. As Jane Lindskold wrote, 'The greatest strength of Fate of the Red Queen is its world-building, from which both plot and characters arise organically.' This short story stands on it's own, an imagined reality that may or may not come after this novel—with an incredibly strong woman. It shares a reality that comes far too close for far too many women, of harassment and misogyny and one the author struggles to understand. All she can say is, 'Be at peace, good soul.'

I was looking for the haunting *xidachene* of my sister Sonalie when I heard faint laughter among the high stacked stone tombs. I turned a corner to discover a surprising terrace: the ruins of an old rail yard that had once given entrance to gardens, before they became overwhelmed by the dead. Among the weeds and rusted tracks was a strange rug house. Sunlight brought out old colors in the bare patches of tough weft and in the fraying edges of the roof. The soft, colorful glory for years of trodding feet now served as a ceiling.

More laughter and giggles and the edge of the rug lifted. Two small faces stared at me, a well-dressed stranger, though not much richer than they. They grew still, but fear was gone from their eyes, leached out by their surroundings.

"Hello," I said.

The children let the rug fall back over the table legs. The table, too, was upside down, giving an edge against both damp ground and the heavy rains that had just left us.

The brief view inside revealed three narrow beds in that strange house. They were all in one big pile, but there were three different worn blankets—red, blue, green—so, I assumed, that the occupants might have their own sense of place. I almost envied them, since I was wearing my sister's clothes, working at her old job, haunted by her *xidachene*. I'd grown up in a slum for servants, in a city where the destitute used stone tombs for homes, or a mausoleum if they were lucky.

This was a very poor house. This little rug house made of cast-off furniture would be no protection from the rain. Rain had not washed away the smell of cat urine, surprising to smell in a place that stank of death and refuse.

Silence from the rug house slowly turned into whispers, rising to talk and more giggles as I made my way past. A gaunt woman in ragged robes walked towards me. Her gaze was vacant—like the ghosts I expected to see.

That's me, I thought, for a moment, *Dying from the curse of my beloved, dead sister.*

A burst of bright laughter from the rug house and the woman's gaunt face transformed it from dying to alive. I had not that peace.

I should not have come in the day. The only dead I could see were safely in their tombs. The noise of the living, including the tinny sound of an ancient sing-song machine, would have driven them away even without the strings of lights that would no doubt be lit up at sunset. I found only the living, paid to pay respect to the dead their families had no time for. It was probably safer than the shanty towns by the river, where the landlords kept tenants in debt, and the flooding took the rest away.

This place could use a rising river to take away the filth piled between the isles of the tombs. Even the residents refused to walk through their own trash, building rickety, one-plank bridges from one rising row of stacked tombs to another. As I walked along the edge of one stack of tombs, six or more tombs high—I could not tell with the years of refuse piled below—I heard noises of yet more music and watched a family eat a meal over one lone tomb, sitting around it as if a tomb was better table than one that had become a floor and walls to a rug house. Ancient tombs, cracked open by time, had been swept clean of ash and dust and dead, and turned into storage, or cramped bedrooms.

A frail, old woman walked past me. With swollen joints crabbing her fingers she knocked on a tomb with a near passive gesture of acknowledgement. I was sure it was something she was paid to do, and had lost all meaning, but then she spoke to the dead as if to a friend and neighbor. I caught my breath, wondering if she could see the person whose grave she tended.

It did not matter. I did not see any *xidachene,* even my sister Sonalie. I had not yet found her tomb. I felt weakened by her loss, something beyond grief. Someday soon I would be like her. Soulless, dead, and still a servant—a slave to a tormentor's whim.

I went back to my home, the rooms I had inherited from her—along with her noisy roommates—when I was old enough to scrub floors of the temple and had inherited her job. I bathed off the stink of the cemetery, wrapped myself in the many layers required by my role, and made my way to work. I did not have to walk far. The building I lived in was a block away from the back of the great temple that I cleaned.

The main hall was gleaming. I tended it anyway.

White marble floors and pillars lifted arches to a gilt ceiling. Rows and rows of pillars with hints of red accents in their carved designs all echoed an ancient queen giving the undead life or death.

The temple was empty between times of prayer, and so I could take the time to clean one row of pillars each day. When the row gleamed brighter than before, I put away my ladder and then went to work on cleaning the morning's foot prints from the floor. I scrubbed a patterned border by the dais with its red stylized footprints of ancient queen and daughter. I polished them until they gleamed like rubies in the white.

"Gazev?"

I sat up on my heels and looked to see an underpriest standing near.

"Yes?" I asked.

"You clean the floor as if praying," Timez said with a smile.

I did not smile back, but said, "If I do, then it is only for the good that I pray."

"I commend you," he said, looking down at me. He paused a moment. "If you desire, you can sit in the nun's alcove and hear the prayers this evening."

I looked at the red screen to the side of the grand hall. I thought of the rumors. Had my sister seen the inside of that sanctum? How often? Once women had ruled this country, but now if women came to worship they were hidden from view. Few women, if any, came in the afternoons, however. They must prepare the evening meal.

I would be alone there.

Perhaps.

"Thank you for the honor," I said. I looked down at my bucket and my pruned, red hands. "I must go home as soon as I am done."

"A pity. Another time?"

I nodded. "Yes. Perhaps I would find it interesting to hear your prayers."

He was new, so my sister could not have known him. I wondered if he knew how often older priests invited the women servants into the old nun's hall. Thus far, I only had the proof of rumors and whispers of older women who could have used the sound of children's laughter—in a graveyard or otherwise. All echoed the whispered truths of how my sister had died, and why.

"Lord Khapan is to say them," he said. "It is a rare service. If you can stay, we would not be disturbed there."

I took a deep breath. It seemed the rumors must be true.

I shook my head, looking at the bucket of soiled water by my knees. "Forgive me, but my duty lies elsewhere tonight."

He put a hand on my shoulder. "Do not reject an opportunity that might do you some good, Gazev." His hand was light. "You work hard for the pleasure of others. Come to hear the prayers."

"I am sorry, but I am obligated tonight," I said, looking up at him.

Haphed, an overpriest, walked towards us. Leering. Timez, seeing the man's face, took his hand off my shoulder as if burnt. His face flamed.

"Forgive me," he said, and turned. His robes snapped as he stalked away.

I contemplated his retreating back. Perhaps I would like to hear his prayers, after all. Haphed leered at me until he was past. I do not know why. He'd said to me once, "You are not as pretty as your sister, but I guess we only need you to clean the floor." He'd also said something about not needing to see my face.

I went home, took off my clothes, including that which wrapped my hair, and much of my head. It was a wonder to me that a holy man like Haphed might see a woman under all those formless layers—even one less pretty than my beautiful sister, Sonalie, whose name echoed that of a royal daughter, and with beauty to match.

Earlier I'd bathed to take off the stench of rotting refuse in the land of the dead and those that lived with them. Now I bathed to remove the weight of men's eyes. Even alone, feeling the burden of shame—my own, and my sister's—I covered myself with my hands, as I stepped into my bath. I shrank under the gaze of the elder priest. It lingered. I'd known of his gaze long before I worked at the temple, hinted at, whispered about at her death.

I'd inherited her rooms, her work, and the years of their gaze upon her beautiful, bent shoulders. My parents might have prevented me, but what else do servants do?

Once clean, I put on dark clothes. My sister's roommates were cooking, talking, and not watching the bright colors of the movie box one of them had been given. Apparently they had no other plans for their night. I climbed up to the roof above my room to escape the cacophony. I was not allowed here, but I could not bear the noise they made. I pulled out my hidden prayer matt and cushion. I had sat here for years, watching the sunset to meditate and pray while many feet brought dirt onto floors I'd just cleaned.

I'd only recently noticed those living beyond the edge of the city in the graveyards. I could see them from here. Surrounding and intermingled trees hid much of the ancient stone tombs from view during the day. Their work fires and lights came alive with the stars that grew bright in the growing dark.

I prayed, hearing the echoes of prayers from the temple behind me, and then climbed back down to my rooms. I donned my dark veils and went back out into the night, escaping the teasing of the two women who shared the space. Their rooms, clothes, and interests felt garish to me. I'd long since learned how they'd embraced that uneven attention that had tormented my sister to death. They believed these gaudy gifts were proof of attention, not treats to the servants so they'd behave. For a brief moment I felt Timez's smooth hand on my shoulder as I knelt before him looking at my hands rough from scrubbing.

I did not care what they thought. They assumed assignation. I only thought that perhaps this time I would see what I had not during the day when the living crowded out the dead in their own homes. If I returned, as I had been doing whenever I could, eventually I might find the tomb of my sister.

Years past, when Sonalie would visit and stay the night, she'd told me that the *xidachene* came out at night. They were trapped souls. These souls did not walk the cities or jungles, as the lore once said. They were people with teeth red from the blood and brains of those they'd killed to protect their graves.

There was no jungle here, now, but a city. The ancient graveyard was not overcome with jungle growth and vine, but by people with their strings of half broken lights and screeching music that rivaled the screeches and howls no longer heard here. Tinny tunes, broken songs, movies half seen with white noise garbling the filmed features, sounds of dry, tired humping—the living engaging in life.

With the burdens of my sister's death I could see what time had turned zombie people into: ghosts hiding from light and people's pretense. I still hoped I would see her, finally, feeding on me, slowly draining my soul because no old woman knocked on her tomb to say, "Hello! We remember you." Even if the woman couldn't remember the dead person's name. Sonalie. Or even, perhaps, Gazev. Me.

However, none of the *xidachene* dead that I could see, or sense, seemed to feed on the living. Perhaps because these living gave the only acknowledgement of their past, scant and cursory as it often must be.

I did not know where my sister was entombed. How could I tell her, if I never found her tomb, that I remembered her? I did not want to carry the burden of her curse. I still loved her.

There weren't as many soulless dead here as I had expected. I thought there would be more *xidachene*. Not finding my sister, as I'd hoped, I wandered back to the city.

Not wanting to go home to noise and talk that would last till the wee hours of the morning—past the point of my exhaustion—I walked. My feet found their way to where I worked every day. I found myself in the temple, empty of prayers and people.

It was quiet. Moon and clouds turned the white floors into shifting silver like the ocean. Without my sponge or broom, I felt too exposed in this great hall. I went to the nuns' rooms. The weak light still gleamed through the red, painted lattice into the gloom of the room. I could make out the benches rising along the tiers that allowed women to pray and see the priests' raised pulpit below. I went to the back where I could kneel and bow without a sponge to scrub the floor, only my prayers.

I looked up at a sound like a sigh. There she was. Sonalie. The *xidachene* that was slowly killing me. I trembled, because now in a sudden glow of unhidden moon, I could see the dead wandering the temple hall below, as well as in this room. There were more here than in the graveyard.

"Sister," I said.

She looked at me, silent.

As if moving through eons, or the vast distance between dead and living, she spoke, "Why did you come?"

"I could not find your grave."

"I did not die there."

I looked around the room. "You did not die here." I knew that much. They had not told me much; I had been so young. I did know that.

"They took my body away here, and then punished me for it."

"Who did?"

"It does not matter. In one blow, trying to take my life and body into my own hands, I joined them in my torment."

That blow, I knew, had been her death.

In the moonlight, she was gaunt, and rotting, as if eaten from within. Her teeth were not red, like legends say. And I knew I'd been wrong. She was cursed I could see, and I was dying as well, but she was not feeding on me. I wanted to ask her why I was dying.

Other *xidachene* wandered around this gallery and the hall below. They moaned and whispered with papery sounds. Then I heard a mockery of prayer from the raised pulpit in the hall. A strange sound that made the hair on my arms raise as it scraped over the prayers.

"He is tormented by being a servant to the wrong gods—not the ones he said his words to to obey—and only just good enough to be pained that he joined his tormentors and became one. He eats, like they did, upon his own flesh and soul, and is tortured more because of his pride for feasting upon mine."

Guilt, apparently, in the afterlife. However, her words disturbed me. I knew that this man—and probably others—had not been cannibals. They had fed upon her all the same, using her body as they used those of my roommates. I wondered if she'd killed him. There were rumors about this as well.

I looked at my sister, consumed from within. Guilt was not less ravaging than shame.

A sound came into the hall, and the strange tones of the *xidachene* priest were stilled. All the shuffling movement and moans of the dead faded. Sonalie and I walked to the lattice.

Timez prayed in the hall. He did not take the stairs up to the pulpit, so he could be better heard. Who was there to hear him, but the Divine? The ancient queen? No one, but me. And the *xidachene*. He did not know this. He merely came, at night, to pray. He did not see or sense the dead that slowly encircled him, unable to keep away from the bright tones of his words. I felt the draw as well, my hands gripping the lattice until it bit into my hands.

We were in the queen's ancient temple, in a room that honored her past as a woman of faith, a queen who had saved the dead from endless dying. We listened to a man's honest prayers.

A *xidachene* touched Timez's shoulder. It was so old, I could not tell if it was a man or woman. Something in the face was familiar, an echo of a dead look. I remembered the woman walking to a rug house, and the sound of children's laughter in a cemetery. A place where a woman's living deadness could transform with sparkling laughter.

The *xidachene's* voice joined that of the young underpriest, his hand so light upon Timez's shoulder. I could hear its hollow voice echo the prayers.

Sonalie said, "He is dead, and undead. I am dead, and undead, denied my own body, and trapped inside it. As I lived, so am I now, dead, and dying. Always dying."

The *xidachene's* face transformed with the prayers. Then he disappeared.

I gasped.

"It's not as simple as that," Sonalie said.

I asked my sister, "Can't you save yourself? Find a final freedom? As he did?"

She shook her head. "That is only a choice of the living."

I knew that she was indeed cursed, then—and would be for as long as she held onto the sense of shame that had killed her and consumed her in death.

She turned to me. "I can save you. You must choose, now. Before it is too late. You already carry burdens that are not your own," she said. "You must give them back to me."

"They are the last of you!" I said, realizing I no longer wanted to let her go. I wanted to keep these deadly burdens for her. The terrible pain and shame she'd carried, that I'd put upon my own shoulders as well; taking her job and seeing what it had done to her, and was trying to do to me.

She reached for me, grabbing hold of what I could not see. She looked at what she held, and then nodded. "Yes, I see. It is not only me you cling to; they begin to watch you now. Let me go to feed upon my past, and ask you: Who owns your body? And like those two different priests down there, who owns your soul?"

Timez's prayers filled the grand hall like the moonlight, making the marble and gilding gleam and deepening the lines of carved reliefs. My fingers interlaced the wooden lattice, and I watched my sister, and one by one all the tormented *xidachene* fade from view.

The bright sounds of one man's prayers filled the space.

And then my voice joined in.

In prayers to the Divine, and an ancient Red Queen, I gave up the burdens of my shame, and that of my sister's. I could feel the joy of bright laughter that filled the space. That of the living, and that of the dying now alive. Maybe that of the dying now dead.

It was not as simple as that, I knew, but still....

"Be at peace, good soul," I said.

THANK YOU TO OUR SUPPORTERS

Many thanks to our patrons and supporters, especially:

**Stephanie Johnston • Anna O'Brien
Cathrin Hagey • S Naomi Scott
Natalie Weizenbaum • Siobhan Beeman**

**Emily Anderson • Felicia OSullivan • J'nae Spano
Katherine Montalto • Kennon Hulett • Martin Cohen
Salomao Becker • Shannon White • Shelly Jones
Tamara Rutledge • Tory Hoke • Bonnie Warford**

**Carly Racklin • Charlotte Nash-Stewart
GriffinFire • Isabel Cañas • Jen G • Jocelyn Actual
Karen Anderson • Kayla • Liz Warner
Maria Haskins • Suzanne Thackston**

Want to see your name here? Become a patron!
patreon.com/lunastation

About the Cover Artist

Leesha Hannigan is a fantasy illustrator, known for her work on Dungeons and Dragons.

Throughout her career, Leesha has primarily worked in the video game and tabletop industries, as well as producing cover art for several fantasy novels. Leesha's artwork has been featured in various publications, such as Spectrum and ImagineFX.

Leesha loves nothing more than surrounding herself in nature, and her love of animals, light and colour shines through in her work.

You can find more of her work at:

leeshahannigan.com

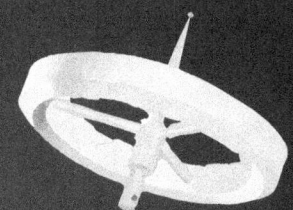

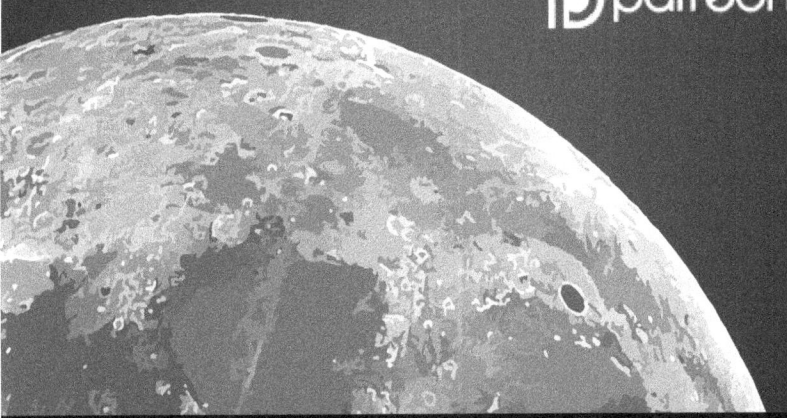